Castleton

A Novel by

TRAY BURCH

First Edition
ISBN: [979-8-9989769-0-2]
Printed in the United States of America

For Jim
Thank you for igniting the passion in me to write.

CHAPTER ONE — *Fireworks & Frosting*

The town of Castleton, New England, woke with the rise of the summer sun. Church steeples stood tall, overlooking white picket fences lining manicured lawns. American flags fluttered proudly from the front porches of colonial homes. Seagulls soared above Raven Lake, painting another postcard day.

It was the Fourth of July, and Castleton—like clockwork—was preparing for a day of festivities. Town officials blocked off streets for the parade, while neighbors prepped for celebrations on every corner.

A local paperboy tossed newspapers down a suburban street, one landing perfectly on the doorstep of a charming colonial—just as the front door opened.

E.J. stepped out wearing his Castleton High tee and a pair of running shorts. He was the All-American boy next door—the kind who'd mow your lawn without being asked and still make it to football practice on time.

Then he stepped off the porch and into the morning light... and that was when you noticed the rest of him.

The sunlight sculpted every inch of his frame with cinematic precision. His shirt clung to broad shoulders, but the unusual July heat pushed him to peel it off, revealing abs carved from early runs and late-night lifts. His body wasn't for show—it was quiet proof of discipline.

His feet hit the pavement, jogging down the sidewalk. As he passed a neatly kept Craftsman home, sprinklers sputtered to life beside him. Just then, a red Honda Civic pulled into the driveway.

Inside that very Craftsman, Charli XCX's "Boys" played from Maria's phone as she piped thick white frosting onto red, white, and blue cupcakes fresh from the oven. The morning sun streamed through the window, casting a soft glow over her teenage features. Her long black hair spilled over one shoulder—a trait inherited from her dad's Latin roots.

The kitchen smelled like sugar, butter, and maybe a little too much vanilla extract—but to Maria, it was just right.

She leaned in to frost the next cupcake, but a knock at the kitchen door made her hand twitch.

Before she could turn around, just as expected, Sam entered from outside, singing along to the music playing from her phone. Sunglasses on his head, tank top bright, iced coffee in hand—full summer sass.

"Okay, Betty Crocker," he quipped, grinning as Maria rolled her eyes.

"You're late."

"I'm *fashionably* late," he shot back, stealing a cupcake without shame. "Besides, I brought you a gift: my mother's car. She handed me the keys to the Civic like it was a trust exercise. That woman is either evolving... or surrendering."

"If I know Aunt Jessica, I'd bet on surrendering when it comes to you."

Sam took a dramatic bite of the cupcake. "Mmm. Patriotic and diabetic."

They both laughed—the kind that only comes from a lifetime of shared sleepovers and whispered secrets. Cousins, technically. Best friends, truly.

Across town, the same beat pulsed faintly from someone's phone, following Castleton into its choreographed morning.

On the front lawn of Castleton High School, home of the Hellcats, the cheer squad was in full formation. Heather, captain since sophomore year, popped her gum and barked a count.

"Five, six, seven, eight—and lift!"

Pom-poms shimmered in the sun as the pyramid rose—then toppled. Heather didn't flinch. She just flipped her ponytail like it had an attitude of its own.

"Again. I want these moves tighter than my mom's Botox schedule."

Paige, co-captain and the squad's voice of reason, waved the girls off.

"Break time."

Heather sighed. "Do you think they're ready for tonight?"

"They'll be fine. Just nerves."

Heather was mid-eye roll when she caught sight of him.

E.J. Winthrop. Jogging shirtless, headphones in, tan catching the light. He looked older, leaner—like a boy who'd spent a lonely summer in the gym.

Heather's lips curled into a slow, satisfied smile.

"Holy hell," she murmured. "Is that E.J. Winthrop?"

Paige looked up. "Puberty. It hit him like a truck."

Heather didn't break her gaze. "He can hit me like a truck."

Elsewhere, on a porch that didn't yet feel like home, a moving van was parked in the driveway of a small bungalow with a freshly planted SOLD sign in the yard. Inside, movers shuffled furniture from the truck as a girl sat quietly on the front porch swing, a leather-bound diary resting on her lap.

Molly.

Seventeen, with sun-kissed blonde hair that curled softly at the ends and wide blue eyes that seemed to take in everything at once. She wore denim shorts and a pale yellow tank top, her bare feet brushing the porch as the swing creaked back and forth. A gold locket glinted at her collarbone as she traced its edge absentmindedly.

She was a little anxious. A new town. A new home. A new school.

The air smelled like freshly cut grass and saltwater, and somewhere in the distance, she could hear music, that same beat, and laughter.

There was something promising about that.

"Hey, kiddo," her dad called from the front door, snapping her out of it. "You okay out here?"

"Yeah," she said, turning to smile at him.

He walked over and ruffled her hair before sitting beside her.

"Tonight we're going to check out the fireworks. Maybe even meet some locals—see what Castleton's all about."

Molly nodded, tucking her hair behind her ear. "Mom would've liked it here."

He smiled gently. "Yeah. I think so too."

The movers made a commotion as they struggled with a sofa. Her dad hopped up to help.

Molly returned to her diary, though she didn't write anything. Not yet.

That's when E.J. jogged around the corner, passing right in front of her. He glanced over just in time to lock eyes with Molly, and it felt like time froze for both of them. Molly blinked. Her heart skipped. E.J. blinked back, caught in the same moment.

Not awkward. Just... curious. Suddenly, she was busy thinking about that boy.

Something in his look felt steady, familiar—like the town had just welcomed her in the quietest way possible.

Then, realizing he was staring, E.J. quickly looked away.

He jogged up his front steps as Molly quietly watched her handsome new neighbor disappear inside his home next door.

Later that night, she'd write about the boy next door—and the town that already felt like it was keeping secrets.

Inside the Winthrop house, the AC was heavenly, and the scent of fresh-squeezed OJ clung to the air. E.J. kicked off his shoes and made his way upstairs, pausing outside his younger sister's door.

"Hey," he called softly before knocking. "You up?"

Jane, sixteen and already polished in a crisp white blouse and denim skirt, opened the door. Her ponytail was high and perfect, not a single hair out of place. Her makeup? Subtle, but flawless.

Classic Jane.

"Of course I'm up. It's the Fourth—lots to do today."

E.J. smirked. "Just wanted to make sure you were good, that's all."

"I'm not glass, E.J.—I won't break," she replied, brushing an invisible wrinkle from her skirt.

"I'll catch you later," he said, heading toward his room.

Once his door clicked shut, Jane's smile faltered. She turned back into her room and closed the door.

She moved to her nightstand drawer. Fingers brushed past a notebook and cherry lip gloss... until they curled around a small orange pill bottle.

She popped the cap, tapped two pills out, and swallowed them dry.

She stood, adjusted her ponytail in the mirror... and whispered to her reflection:

"Let the fireworks begin."

CHAPTER TWO — *Secret Sparks*

As the day eased into evening, the heart of Castleton began to pulse with excitement. Along Main Street, red, white, and blue streamers fluttered with patriotic pride from every lamppost. Families gathered along sidewalks, waving tiny flags, with little kids perched on shoulders. The scent of grilled hot dogs and kettle corn drifted through the air as the town buzzed with anticipation.

At the front of the Fourth of July parade, sirens blared as Castleton's fire trucks rolled by, lights flashing and candy flying from smiling volunteers on the back. Children scrambled with open hands, their laughter echoing through the crowd.

The Castleton High Marching Band followed not far behind, horns and drums creating a rhythm that got the whole crowd moving. At the judging station near the gazebo, the cheer squad performed their routine with flawless precision. Pom-poms shimmered like fireworks as they nailed their final stunt, drawing cheers and applause. Heather turned to Paige with a sense of pride.

By the time the parade filtered toward Raven Lake, the sun began to fade. At the lakeside fairgrounds, clusters of white tents had popped up beneath strings of twinkling lights. Vendors sold everything from traditional funnel cakes and corn dogs to New England-style lobster rolls, a local specialty. On the main stage, a local band played upbeat music that kept the crowd moving.

At one of the busiest stands, a group of students—including Maria and Sam—stood behind an assortment of baked goods. Maria's cupcakes were proudly displayed. A sign taped to the table read: *Support Mrs. Thayer's Performing Arts Program!*

Sam leaned on the edge of the table, sipping lemonade as he scanned the crowd.

"Your cupcakes were a hit," he said, nodding at the nearly empty trays. "We're almost sold out."

Maria smiled, brushing a few crumbs off the table, as Sam's phone vibrated in his pocket. He slid it out to look at it. Maria noticed—he had been on it all day.

Sam's posture shifted, his eyes lighting up at a text. His smile changed... softer. More vulnerable.

"What's up?" she asked.

"Nothing," he said quickly, slipping the phone back into his pocket. "I just... have somewhere I need to be."

Maria raised an eyebrow. "Or someone you need to see?"

She knew him too well.

Sam's eyes sparkled. "In due time, you'll find out."

Maria watched him a beat longer than necessary. It wasn't his words—it was the way he said them. Almost hopeful. This wasn't how he acted for a normal hookup. This felt different... if it was even a hookup, she wondered—but she didn't push it.

"Go," she said, without the much-needed tea. "Be mysterious."

Sam grinned. "Always."

Before she could think more about it, Maria was approached by another customer hoping to snag one of the last few cupcakes she had baked.

At the "Dunk the Hunk" booth, shirtless local athletes—many from Castleton High's football team—took their turns on the seat above the tank, the water below glistening under the string lights. Suddenly, a broad-shouldered junior was knocked in with a loud—

SPLASH!

Heather clapped her hands with excitement from her post beside the booth—a volunteer duty she enjoyed a bit too much.

"Mmm, thank you, gravity," she purred, watching as Dillon, Castleton High's star linebacker, stood dripping wet. His brown skin glistened as he smiled for the cheering crowd.

Paige jogged up to Heather, breathless. "Hey, I can't find Tyler. He's up next."

Heather whipped her ponytail with precision. "Well, that's disappointing."

Then she spotted him… again… E.J., wandering through the crowd in the distance.

"I have a replacement," Heather said, already slinking toward him.

Paige raised a brow. "You're not serious."

"I'm dead serious."

"He'd never do it."

"Watch me," Heather said, already on the move.

E.J. noticed her a second too late.

"E.J.," she said sweetly. "Hope you've been well. I need you desperately."

He eyed the nearby booth. "The dunk booth?"

Heather batted her lashes. "You'd be helping a good cause. All proceeds go to charity. And besides… shirtless looks good on you."

E.J. smiled, flattered and a little embarrassed. "Actually, I'm looking for my sister, Jane. I was just about to text her."

"She's a big girl," Heather said, brushing it off. "You're not the kind of guy who turns down a good deed, right?"

E.J. hesitated, eyes flicking back toward the crowd. Jane wasn't visible, but Heather was—staring up at him with a challenge in her eyes.

Maybe it was harmless. Maybe Jane needed space. Maybe…

He sighed. "Fine."

Heather beamed as she grabbed his hand and hurried him over to the booth.

"Wait—right now?" E.J. asked bashfully as Heather helped him remove his shirt.

Paige watched from the side of the booth. She should've known better than to underestimate Heather's ability to get what she wanted. That was one of her trademarks, Paige thought—having everything. And deep down, Paige kind of wanted to be her.

As E.J. walked over to the tank and began settling onto the seat, Heather approached Paige.

"By the end of the night," she whispered, "E.J. Winthrop will be mine."

Paige eyed Heather, wondering just how far she would go.

Underneath the night sky, Molly walked beside her father, weaving through the crowd, tents, and vendor booths—a father-daughter date of sorts.

"Mr. Lockhart!" a man called from the crowd.

Her dad turned toward the voice, spotting his new business partner, Sullivan O'Brien.

"I see my new business partner is settling in well," Sullivan said, smiling as he extended a hand.

As her dad and Mr. O'Brien launched into business talk, Molly drifted away, leaving her dad to dive in. Just as she turned the corner, she saw him... again.

E.J. Winthrop. Sitting above the dunk tank, arms folded across his bare chest, a smile playing on his face as a little kid failed to hit the target.

Then, he glanced over and noticed her. She now had his full attention.

Molly smiled, her blue eyes wide. E.J. smiled back—a smile that could've melted her heart.

Suddenly a nudge on Molly's arm distracted her. An older woman with a sly smile.

"Give it a shot, honey."

At first hesitant, Molly stepped forward as the kid handed her the ball. Her heart fluttered. She noticed the target, then made eye contact with E.J.

They laughed.

She had never done anything like this.

Eyes back on the target. She aimed... and hit it dead center.

SPLASH!

E.J. plunged into the tank as the crowd cheered. Molly ran toward the tank as he resurfaced, sputtering and laughing.

As he stepped out, dripping wet, Heather approached—like clockwork—with a towel.

"Thanks, Heather," E.J. said, taking it as water slid down his chest.

"Not bad," he said to Molly.

"Beginner's luck," she teased.

"Or deadly precision," he countered.

Their banter flowed effortlessly—like they'd known each other for years. Heather backed off as Paige watched from the side, ever observant.

E.J. and Molly moved together instinctively, drawn like magnets.

Heather watched from a distance, her smile completely vanished.

Who is this new girl? she wondered.

In the woods just beyond the fairgrounds, moonlight streamed through the trees. The only sound was faint music from the festivities.

Sam stood alone, texting.

Where are you? he typed.

Rustling.

The sound of a twig breaking made Sam turn. A figure stepped out of the shadows.

It was Tyler. Varsity jacket on.

"You came," Sam said.

"Of course I did," Tyler replied, stepping close. "Though I feel bad for leaving Heather hanging. I was supposed to be at the dunk booth."

Sam stepped closer, slowly. "Do you know what it feels like to have to pretend this isn't a thing?"

Tyler stayed silent.

Sam closed the gap.

Then-

A kiss. Quiet. Familiar.

Their eyes met. They wanted each other.

"I don't want to be a secret anymore," Sam whispered.

Tyler flinched. "Come on, you know that's not possible. Not right now."

Sam's voice broke just a little. "I just wish, Ty."

Tyler looked at him like it hurt to breathe.

Then... he kissed Sam again—harder. Desperate. Needing.

Sam responded with equal fire, hands sliding beneath Tyler's shirt. Wanting more. Now. He traced every ridge of Tyler's torso.

They stumbled until Tyler's back hit a tree. Sam pinned him there, lips on his neck, hands moving fast.

A button popped. Then fingers reached for the zipper—brushing against what was already hard beneath.

When—

BOOM!

The first firework exploded overhead, colors spraying above the treetops. Then another—purple... blue...

Sam paused, eyes flicking to the sky, then back to Tyler, his breath hot and fast.

The fireworks crackled above Raven Lake—loud, bright, and breathtaking. Colorful bursts shimmered across the water, their reflections dancing on the surface.

In the crowd, Molly stood beside E.J., their shoulders just brushing. Neither said much—but they didn't need to.

As Molly watched each spark, E.J. looked over at her. And for a moment, the fireworks seemed quieter—like the world had lowered its volume just for them.

"Pretty cool, huh?" he said, not taking his eyes off her.

She glanced at him, smiling gently. "It's perfect."

He smiled as Molly tucked a piece of hair behind her ear, her eyes lingering on him. She felt it—that magnetic pull again, like earlier on the porch.

E.J. shifted slightly closer. "Glad you moved here," he said softly, almost like he hadn't meant to say it out loud.

Molly's heart skipped. "Me too," she whispered.

A firework bloomed overhead—an enormous golden one, glittering in slow motion. E.J. reached down, his hand brushing hers.

Molly let her fingers slide into his, feeling comfort.

In the distance, Heather watched, arms crossed, a look of frustration.

E.J. and that girl. That girl who came out of nowhere and already had his attention.

Paige approached beside her. "You okay?"

Heather didn't answer.

Finally, she spoke. "Who the hell is she?"

"I think," Paige said carefully, "you've got competition."

Heather's jaw tightened. "Not for long."

Another firework exploded above them—this one red. Sharp. Fast. Like a warning shot.

CHAPTER THREE — *Pink Lies & Private Pain*

The morning sun crept over Castleton, casting a soft golden light across a massive Greek Revival home perched atop a hill, overlooking Raven Lake and most of town—Briarwood Estate.

From the outside, the house looked ready for a *New England Home* cover shoot, with its regal white columns, trimmed hedges, and a cherry-red convertible shining in the driveway.

But inside, the illusion was cracking.

In a perfectly curated pink bedroom—complete with a crystal chandelier and a neon hot pink sign that read *Like, Literally Iconic*—Heather Briarwood slept like royalty.

Wrapped in blush silk sheets, eye mask on, lips parted slightly, she was the picture of spoiled serenity.

Until—

SPLASH!

A wave of cold water hit her square in the face.

She screamed, bolting upright—soaked and sputtering, silk clinging to her like betrayal. She tore off her eye mask and yanked out her earplugs to find her parents standing at the foot of her bed like elegantly dressed demons.

"What the actual HELL?!" she gasped, blinking through dripping lashes.

Her father, in a monogrammed robe, looked sheepish. Her mother, in a lavender tracksuit, oversized sunglasses, and pearls, sipped from a mimosa flute like the whole situation was just terribly inconvenient.

"Don't be so dramatic—we tried to wake you, but you had your earplugs in," her mother explained.

Cutting to the chase, she said flatly, "We're broke."

Heather froze. "Say what now?"

"Broke," her father echoed, with the gravity of a man announcing a death in the family. "The accounts are empty."

Heather laughed, sharp and disbelieving. "This is a joke, right? A sick, twisted—"

"No trust fund. No allowance. No charge accounts," her mother interjected. "Daddy made a few risky investments."

"They were sure things!" her father shouted defensively.

"You're a fool!" her mother corrected, before continuing, "I'm sure we have something to salvage—but Heather, darling, you need to get a job."

"Come again?" Heather blinked. She needed to be sure she heard correctly.

"A J-O-B," her mother spelled out. "Character-building... everyone loves a comeback story."

Mr. and Mrs. Briarwood turned to exit the bedroom, bombshell dropped. As the door clicked shut, it felt like Heather's entire kingdom was falling.

She let out a scream—*a Beverly Hills-level meltdown* that rattled the perfume bottles on her vanity.

Groaning, she collapsed back into the damp pillows, already dreading the idea of doing anything so *pedestrian* as applying for jobs.

What was she supposed to do—bag groceries?

Her phone buzzed on the nightstand. A push notification from social media: **Keegan Prescott posted a story**.

Ugh. Of course he was posting another shirtless pic from his parents' infinity pool.

Some people got to have private chefs and bottomless Amex cards while making TikToks about *feeling burnt out*, she thought.

Heather rolled her eyes and turned the screen face down. She had bigger problems than Castleton's favorite nepotism prince.

She stared at the ceiling, pink light glowing overhead, the air feeling heavier than it should.

Another girl stared at a different kind of ceiling. Quieter. Colder. Just as heavy, if not more.

Nearly thirty miles away from Castleton, in a coastal village... the ocean crashed gently onto the shore in a town called Harmony.

Jane, still staring at the ceiling from inside a therapist's office, didn't want to be there at all.

She sat upright in the large chair, adjusting her posture—*gotta keep up appearances*, she thought. The tall, wide windows gave her a beautiful view of the coastline. A moment of escape, but when the office door opened and Dr. Crane entered, reality came crashing back in.

Sure, Jane looked every bit the composed teenager—perfect ponytail, pressed white blouse, posture prim—but her eyes were tired. Not from lack of sleep, but from pretending everything was okay.

Dr. Crane, in a soft cream blazer and stylish glasses, sat across from her, holding a journal in hand—but she rarely wrote in it. She listened more than she spoke. Her energy was calm, unwavering.

"So, Jane," she said gently. "How have things been since our last session?"

"Fine," Jane replied quickly.

Dr. Crane didn't flinch. Her black curls were pinned back, legs crossed in a pencil skirt, the sun hitting her caramel skin in a perfect glow.

"And how does *fine* feel this week?"

Jane's gaze flicked toward the window, watching the Atlantic waves roll in. "It feels like I'm doing what I'm supposed to."

"Supposed to?" Dr. Crane repeated. "For who?"

Jane said nothing. She sat still—but tense.

Dr. Crane paused. Then asked, carefully, "Would you like to talk about Johnny today?"

Jane's voice cracked, just a little. "Why would we talk about him when you know his name is like a knife stabbing me a thousand times over?"

Jane's eyes began to well. She wiped them quickly. She needed to stay strong.

"Because unspoken grief doesn't disappear," Dr. Crane replied. "It just... festers. Beneath the surface."

A long silence settled between them. Jane hated being in the hot seat. Hated being here.

Finally, she whispered, "I don't dream about him anymore."

Dr. Crane nodded, encouraging.

"That should be a good thing, right?" Jane continued—then abruptly shut down. "I'm sorry—I can't do this."

She jumped up and stormed out of the room. Dr. Crane called after her, but Jane was halfway through the lobby. She passed her father without making eye contact.

When Dr. Crane met Mr. Winthrop's gaze, he approached the office door. She didn't sugarcoat it.

"She's still surviving," she said gently. "And survival isn't the same as healing."

Mr. Winthrop looked down, voice cracking. "She used to laugh. Now she barely speaks."

"She's carrying more than she knows how. She needs space to stop pretending she's okay."

Later that day, back in Castleton, Jane stormed into the Winthrop home. Her mother called from the kitchen.

"Jane?"

No answer. Just the sound of footsteps—and a door slamming shut.

Upstairs, Jane moved to her nightstand drawer. Same routine. Pill bottle. Pop the cap. Two pills. Swallow.

She collapsed into her bed, crying silently, her face buried in the pillow, her body rigid.

This was the version of her no one could ever see—except...

A whisper.

"Stop crying."

She knew the voice well. Dizzy, she lifted her head and stared at him.

Johnny.

Kneeling beside her bed, he looked barely older than her.

She whispered, "This is all your fault," almost angry.

Tears streamed down her cheeks as she stared at him—his expression manic.

A blink.

And he was gone.

Maybe he'd never been there at all.

Downstairs, E.J. stepped in through the kitchen door, his T-shirt clinging from a run.

"Jane back?" he asked, grabbing a water from the fridge.

His mom nodded. "Didn't say much."

"She never does anymore," E.J. muttered. "These sessions... I'm not sure they're helping."

"They're with Dr. Crane. She knows what she's doing."

"Yeah, but Harmony isn't exactly neutral ground. I know Dr. Crane's a family friend, but that town... it's where everything broke."

His mom paused, hand resting on the edge of the counter. "You think we should move her sessions here?"

"Maybe. If we're rebuilding, shouldn't we stop dragging her back to the wreckage?"

She studied him for a moment—so steady, so full of weight he didn't deserve.

"You're a good brother," she said, brushing his cheek.

He smiled weakly, trying not to show how tired he was—from the run… and everything else.

Then she changed the subject, lighter. "Have you met the new neighbors yet?"

E.J. looked through the kitchen window just in time to see Molly walking back inside the house next door.

"She seems nice," he said, voice softening—like the thought of her already meant something.

His mom raised a brow as he kept staring.

He caught himself. "Can't wait for dinner, Mom," he said quickly, then headed upstairs.

"Mmhmm," she murmured knowingly.

Next door, in the Lockhart home, Molly lay on her bed, her diary open, music playing softly.

She wrote carefully, her pen gliding across the page:

Mom would've loved it here. This town is so charming, and there's still so much to discover.

And the boy next door? I think I might already be in trouble. He's really cute. The thought of him takes my breath away.

Her phone buzzed.

E.J.: Want to grab ice cream?

Molly smiled, tucking a strand of hair behind her ear.

Molly: I would love to :)

She hopped off her bed, darting to the mirror to fix her messy blonde hair, then slid on her sandals.

The love bug had bitten her.

CHAPTER FOUR — *Whispers at Twilight*

The sun had dipped behind the hills of Castleton, casting the town in pale blue shadows as crickets began their evening chorus. Jane strolled down the long Winthrop driveway. Lately, the mail carrier had been showing up later.

The mailbox creaked as she opened it—bills, coupons, and the latest glossy issue of *Yankee Magazine.*

Behind her, laughter and footsteps approached.

Jane turned, her ponytail swinging, to find E.J. with Molly.

"This is my sister, Jane," E.J. said, his tone light with Molly. "Jane, this is Molly. She just moved in next door."

Molly offered a warm smile. "Hi. It's nice to meet you."

Jane smiled back with a wave. "Welcome to Castleton."

"Thanks for the ice cream," Molly said to E.J., her tone grateful. "It was *so* good."

"Yeah, Brady's has the best ice cream in this part of New England," E.J. replied with a grin.

"I should get home before my dad starts to worry," Molly said, though part of her wished she could stay a little longer.

"Of course," E.J. nodded. "We should get inside too. See you around."

"See you," Molly called as she headed next door.

She paused at her own mailbox as Jane wandered over. Just the two of them now, under a sky where the first stars were beginning to twinkle.

"You two are cute together," Jane said with a soft grin.

Molly laughed. "You think so?"

"Oh yeah," Jane replied. "Our family's been through a lot lately... it's just nice to see E.J. smile like that again."

"I get it," Molly said, her voice quiet, thoughtful. "I know that feeling all too well."

Molly hesitated, then added with more warmth, "Hey, maybe we could hang out sometime? Just us girls."

Jane was surprised. It had been a long time since anyone had asked her that—longer still since she'd said yes.

A slow smile crept in. "Yeah. I'd like that."

The next morning, Castleton's downtown awoke with its usual rhythm, teeing up another sunny day. Heather passed a row of colonial shops and stopped outside Castleton Coffee House. Her oversized sunglasses dipped low as she stared at the "Help Wanted" sign in the window like it was a personal insult.

"You've got to be kidding me," she muttered.

"Looking for a job, or just killing time?"

Heather spun around, startled.

Keegan Prescott leaned against the brick wall beside the shop, tousled dark hair and tanned skin catching the light. Heather clocked his expensive watch—but this time, Keegan wasn't trying to show off. Not with her. The Briarwoods were just as rich... or at least, he still thought so.

He turned to click and lock his black Range Rover before turning back.

"Well, well," he said, his voice like a yawn wrapped in charm. "Look who's slumming it."

Heather groaned. "I'm surprised you're not off in some tropical paradise for summer break."

"I just got back," he replied easily—but for someone surrounded by luxury, he always looked like he'd rather be anywhere else. "Look, I'm throwing a party tomorrow."

"Who's going?" she asked, her interest piqued.

"Does it matter?" He smirked. "You know my parties are legendary. We need one good night before school starts up again. Invite everybody."

She raised a brow. "Let me guess—parents off to the Maldives? Capri?"

"Bingo, place is mine for a while. I'm shocked they haven't linked up with your folks. It's been a while since they got together."

Heather flinched internally at the mention of her parents. Bankruptcy—gross, but Keegan couldn't know.

Switching gears quickly, she said, "Fine. I could use some brainless fun. I'll spread the word."

"Sounds like a plan," Keegan said, already heading inside the shop.

He had barely taken three steps before Heather was pulling out her phone, fingers flying as she posted the details to social media. Anything to take her mind off her problems. Plus, it wouldn't be such a bad idea to reclaim her place in Castleton's social scene. A sense of normalcy—no matter how fake—sounded perfect right now.

Before Keegan could even order his latte, the party invite was already live… the buzz had begun.

CHAPTER FIVE — *Cracks in the Glass*

By 6 p.m. the next day, house music already thumped through the Prescott Estate—a sprawling New England mansion not far from Briarwood. The place oozed old money. Ivy clung to its stone walls, and the grand living room had been cleared for a DJ who kept the beats coming as students from Castleton High—and a few strays from Mill Valley and Harmony—poured in.

Heather and Paige stood near the staircase, effortlessly cool in that curated-but-casual way. They sipped spiked pink lemonade from red cups.

Keegan approached from behind, sunglasses perched on his head, a drink in hand.

"Look at this," he said, smirking. "Place looks alive again."

Heather smiled. Paige chimed in, "You always have the best parties."

Keegan raised his cup. "Thanks for making it worth it."

Then he was gone—vanishing into the crowd to mingle like a shadow slipping through light.

Heather scanned the room—eyes sharp, calculating. And then, like clockwork, she saw them.

E.J., Molly, and Jane walked in together.

Time slowed.

Her fingers tightened around her cup, a flicker of annoyance and opportunity blooming in her chest.

"Oh no," Paige muttered. "I see the wheels turning."

Heather's pink-glossed lips curled into a smile that didn't quite reach her eyes. "I'm just being polite. Welcoming the new girl."

She flipped her hair and gave Paige a pointed look. "It's only right. Don't you think?"

Before Paige could answer, Heather was already moving—gliding through the party with purpose, not urgency.

"Molly, right?" she said, materializing at their side. "I don't think we've officially met. I'm Heather."

Molly smiled, a little wary. "Hi."

"Come on, I want to introduce you to some people," Heather beamed, looping her arm through Molly's like they were old friends.

Molly glanced back at E.J. and Jane, unsure. "Sure," she said politely.

E.J. watched them disappear into the crowd, brows knitting. "Wait, what?"

Paige appeared beside him. "Isn't it sweet Heather wants to play tour guide?"

"Yeah," E.J. said flatly, already weaving through the crowd to follow. "Sweet."

Jane shot Paige a glare and trailed after him.

The party pulsed around them—music, lights, voices blurring into one constant beat.

Across the room, Maria and Sam had arrived, slipping through the noise like they'd done it a hundred times.

They sipped punch near a sliding glass door overlooking the pool.

Then Sam saw him.

Outside—Tyler. Surrounded by teammates, red cups in hand.

Their eyes met.

Sam smiled and lifted a hand.

Tyler looked away. Like he hadn't seen him at all.

Sam's smile faltered. "Maybe I shouldn't have come," he said quietly, already turning.

Maria glanced through the glass doors. Tyler looked away—cowardly. Maria, already piecing the puzzle followed after Sam.

Jane moved from room to room, scanning faces. Still no EJ… No Molly.

She turned, spotting a punch bowl.

She made her way over, filling a cup with punch.

Then—

She turned and collided with someone.

Red punch splashed across their shirt.

"Sorry—" The voice froze.

Jane did too.

Tate.

A face from a life she'd buried.

"Jane?" he said, stunned.

Her heart didn't skip—it seized.

"What are you doing here?" she asked, sharp.

"My cousin knows Keegan. I didn't know you'd be here."

She snatched a handful of napkins, dabbing at her shirt, trying to stay composed.

"Don't say anything," she hissed.

"I won't," he said quickly.

"Seriously." Her voice dropped, threatening. "No one can know about Harmony. Not after what happened with Johnny."

Tate nodded, but she was already gone, swallowed by the crowd, heart hammering.

The music pounded, crowds winding through the house, passing a hall tucked away. Inside one of the rooms was a private library—away from the chaos, lit in warm golds. The bass outside was just a thrum. Antique furniture lined the walls like ghosts from another era.

A large oak tree outside cast shifting shadows through the window, landing across Heather and Molly.

"So," Heather said casually, "where exactly are you from?"

"Mill Valley," Molly answered, polite but guarded. "Couple hours from here."

Heather raised a brow. "That tiny place in the middle of nowhere? I don't know how you did it."

Molly gave a shrug. "You get used to it."

"And you moved here with your dad?"

"Yeah."

Heather leaned in, voice honeyed and low. "I guess I'm just surprised. You're really not E.J.'s usual type."

Molly blinked. "He has a type?"

"You're just…" Heather tilted her head. "Simple. Kind of basic, honestly. Like farm-girl-meets-freshman-orientation."

She laughed, hollow and sugar-coated. "Be honest—do you really think a guy like E.J. is into you?" Her voice dropped, cutting. "Or are you just easy?"

Molly's grip tightened around her cup. She didn't react—not in front of Heather.

But the words landed like glass under skin.

Then—

The door opened.

E.J. stepped in, Paige behind him.

His eyes locked on Molly.

"Are you okay?" he asked.

Molly's throat tightened. "I'm fine," she said quickly, brushing past him without looking up.

He turned sharply to Heather. "What did you say to her?"

Heather smiled, all innocence. But E.J. didn't wait. He followed Molly back into the crowd.

"I tried to stall him," Paige muttered. "But whatever you did? You might've just pushed them closer."

Heather's glare could've cracked stone.

At the same time, Molly rushed toward the front doors, blinking fast, trying not to cry.

She didn't see Jane coming the other way—fast and pale.

Jane slipped into the nearest bathroom and locked the door behind her.

She was shaking.

From her pocket: orange pill bottle. Pop. Two pills. Swallow.

She paced. Her thoughts ricocheted like bullets.

Couldn't breathe. Couldn't think.

The bathroom door handle rattled.

"Find another one!" she yelled, voice fraying.

She gripped the sink.

Tick. Tick. Drip.

The faucet leaked. Her heartbeat matched it.

Then—

A **FLASH…**

Jane under a table. Cheer uniform soaked in blood. She didn't know whose. Didn't want to.

Tate's voice beside her: "What's happening?"

She couldn't speak.

Another **flash**—*Dr. Crane's voice echoed, Would you like to talk about Johnny?*

Johnny.

The name tore her open.

Jane came to, back in the bathroom, staring at her reflection in the mirror, trying to bury those memories.

She didn't recognize herself.

Mascara streaked. Lips trembling. Eyes wide and ruined.

Then—

She **SCREAMED!**

A sound from somewhere deep—like her body couldn't hold it anymore.

She swung her fist.

The mirror shattered.

Glass rained down in a thousand glittering shards.

And Jane Winthrop stood in the center of it all—splintered, and finally… broken.

CHAPTER SIX — *Somebody's Watching*

The air outside the Prescott Estate had cooled, a breeze whispering through the tall hedges.

Molly sat on the stone curb just beyond the entrance gates, the laughter and music of the party muffled behind her. She wiped at her cheeks, catching the stray tears still falling.

Then—footsteps.

She turned just as E.J. appeared, his silhouette golden in the last light of day. He was looking for her. Of course he was.

"Molly," he said softly, approaching—his voice grounding her instantly. "You okay?"

She sniffled, gave a shaky smile, tried to play it off. "Yeah. Just needed air."

"You've been crying."

She looked away. He didn't press. He just sat beside her—close, but not pushing.

"Heather," Molly finally said, barely louder than the breeze. "She said some things. Pretty awful things. About me. About... you."

E.J. turned to her, voice quiet but certain. "Whatever she said doesn't matter. I don't care how she sees you. I care about you."

Molly searched his eyes, almost like she was looking for the catch. There wasn't one.

"You mean that?" she asked.

He nodded, brushing his fingers gently against hers. "I do."

Her walls gave in—just a little. She leaned into him, resting her head on his shoulder as the sky deepened and shadows stretched across the road.

It was the calm before something none of them saw coming.

Inside, the party buzzed.

Maria pushed through the crowd, scanning faces. Music pulsed beneath her feet, strobe lights slicing across the room.

"Have you seen Sam?" she asked a guy holding two drinks.

He shook his head.

Then—commotion. A crowd had gathered near a guest bathroom. A girl turned to Maria. "You know what happened?"

"What?" Maria asked, catching sight of shattered glass on the tile —and a thin trail of blood disappearing down the hall.

"There was a scream," the girl added.

A guy nearby nodded. "No one saw who came out."

Maria backed away. She needed to find Sam—now. As more curious partygoers filled the hallway, she slipped back into the crowd.

The guest house loomed over the pool, quieter, darker.

Sam had made his way up to the second level. It was the perfect escape—quiet, still. The music from the main house felt distant, like a heartbeat underwater.

He walked slowly down the hallway, eyes on his phone. Scrolling. Distracting. Pretending tonight hadn't started unraveling the moment Tyler looked away.

"Sam."

He froze. Turned.

Tyler.

He must've followed him.

"Seriously?" Sam said, voice tight. "Now you see me? Like I'm not some ghost?"

Tyler glanced over his shoulder, then stepped closer. "I'm sorry."

He reached for Sam's hand.

Sam pulled back. "You don't want anyone to know we're together —so why are you here?"

"Come on," Tyler muttered.

Tyler moved past him, opened the door to a guest suite, and pulled Sam inside before he could protest. The door clicked shut.

Just then—a shadow moved quietly up the stairs.

Inside the suite, Tyler paced. Sam set his phone on the glass coffee table.

"I didn't come here to fight," Tyler said. "I just... I didn't know what to do earlier. You don't get it. I can't be out. Not right now. My dad would lose it. My teammates would never let it go."

Sam's voice cracked. "So you pretend I don't exist?"

"No." Tyler stepped toward him. "I just need time. Please."

Sam stared at him. "I don't want to be your secret."

"But you're the only person I want."

Then—Tyler kissed him.

Sam froze.

Then pulled away.

Too much. Too fast.

Tyler stood still, uncertain.

Sam wanted to stay strong. To say no. But the truth was... he wanted Tyler too.

He stepped forward and kissed him back—deeper, fiercer. Hands moved faster. Heat blurred thoughts.

Then—

A shadow broke the moment.

They turned.

Tyler's hands still gripping Sam's waist.

Dillon stood in the doorway.

Phone raised. Recording.

"Well, well..." he smirked. "Look what we have here."

Tyler froze. Jaw clenched.

Then instinct took over.

Tyler shoved Sam—hard.

Sam stumbled backward.

CRASH!

The coffee table shattered.

Glass. Silence.

"Sam!" Tyler gasped, rushing forward.

But it was too late.

Sam wasn't moving. A cut on his forehead. Blood trickling. Stillness.

Tyler turned, breath ragged.

"He came onto me," he blurted. "You saw it."

Dillon stared at the glass. At Sam.

His smirk vanished.

"Jesus, Ty... what the hell did you do?"

Tyler didn't answer.

Silence.

Below them, the music kept playing.

Like the world hadn't just changed.

But it had.

CHAPTER SEVEN — *Afterglow*

The hospital lights buzzed overhead—harsh and sterile. Sam blinked groggily, a dull ache pressing behind his eyes.

"Hey," Maria whispered, her voice soft with emotion.

He turned toward her. She sat beside his bed, sleeves tugged over her hands.

"Aunt Jessica's on her way," she said. "You were rushed here from the party. You've been out for a while."

Sam tried to sit up. Pain flared sharp across his ribs. He grimaced. "The party...?"

Maria nodded, glancing toward the small hospital window that looked into the hallway. Tyler and Dillon paced outside—twin figures of restless guilt.

"They've been here since you arrived," she said. "They found you."

Memories flickered in Sam's mind—Tyler's panicked voice, the crash, his own heartbeat thundering in his ears.

"Tyler..." Sam whispered.

Maria's face shifted, suspicion sharp. "Tyler... he had something to do with this, didn't he?" Her anger rising.

Sam swallowed hard. "No," he said, voice barely audible. "It's all blurry."

Maria cooled down. She reached for his hand—but stopped herself short.

"Sorry," she murmured. "You need to rest."

In the hallway, Tyler leaned back against the wall, arms folded tight across his chest.

"Did you delete it?" he asked Dillon under his breath.

Dillon didn't answer right away. He lifted his head, studying Tyler carefully.

"Are you gay?"

Tyler stiffened. "No."

Dillon raised an eyebrow.

Before either could say more, the door to the hospital room flung open.

Maria stormed out, eyes blazing. Without warning, she shoved Tyler hard in the chest—not enough to move him, but enough to make her fury known.

"This is your fault!" she snapped. "I know it!"

Tyler didn't move. He didn't speak. He just stood there, jaw locked, absorbing the blows.

Maria swung again, fists hitting like raindrops, her voice breaking with each hit.

"Maria!"

E.J.'s voice cut through the tension. He and Molly rounded the corner, eyes wide with alarm.

E.J. was at Maria's side in an instant, pulling her back gently, murmuring, "Enough. It's okay."

Maria sagged against him, exhausted sobs spilling into his shoulder.

Tyler turned and walked away without a word, disappearing down the hall.

Dillon watched him go, one hand shoved into his pocket, the other wrapped tightly around his phone.

Across town, a fire crackled on the edge of Raven Lake, flames spitting embers into the night.

Leftovers from Keegan's party gathered near a fire pit for a late-night after-party hangout. Closest to the flames, in a broken circle, sat Heather, Paige, and Keegan—faces flushed from heat and too little sleep.

"Well," Keegan said, stretching his arms overhead, "this night was one for the books."

"No kidding," Paige said, brushing sand from her legs. "Never a dull moment at a Keegan party."

Keegan grinned as he stood. "Gonna grab some drinks from my truck."

He wandered off into the darkness, leaving Paige and Heather alone with the fire.

Heather stared into the flames, the light catching the sharp angles of her face. She spoke without looking up.

"Do you think I'm a bad person?"

Paige blinked, caught off guard. "What?"

Heather hugged her knees tighter, eyes locked on the fire.

"E.J. is definitely hot—that transformation deserves *all* the credit —but things got messy. It was never really about him. It was about Molly. I felt like I needed to win. I couldn't let her—some farm girl from nowhere—show up and one-up me. But I think I turned into a monster for the things I said to her."

Paige hesitated, then said carefully, "I don't think that makes you a bad person. Just... competitive."

Heather gave a tired half-smile. "Yeah. Maybe."

Headlights bumped over the gravel path—Dillon's truck pulling up beside Keegan's.

Dillon hopped out, moving with casual, practiced ease, making his way toward Keegan, who was grabbing beers from his truck bed.

"What's good, brother?" Keegan said, clapping his hand in a quick dap.

Dillon returned it with a tired smirk.

"How's the kid?" Keegan asked

"Sam's awake," Dillon said, helping grab a six-pack. "Looks like he'll be okay."

Keegan leaned back against the tailgate. "You know what happened?"

Dillon hesitated just long enough to answer without words.

"Not really. Everything was a blur."

Keegan didn't push. He nodded once and headed back toward the fire, Dillon following beside him.

Back at the pit, Dillon dropped into an empty chair next to Paige, tossing her a lazy grin.

"Didn't know you were coming," Paige said, smiling brighter than she meant to.

"Guess I needed to unwind," Dillon said easily. His eyes flicked to her. "It's beautiful out here. Beautiful company, too."

Heather rolled her eyes good-naturedly and nudged Keegan. "Come on," she said. "Let's give these two some space."

Keegan let himself be dragged off, disappearing down the lakeshore with Heather.

Somewhere near the fire pit, a beat-up Bluetooth speaker buzzed to life. Beach House's *Lemon Glow* slipped into the air—hypnotic, strobing synth wrapping the lakeshore in a hazy trance.

At the water's edge, Heather turned to Keegan.

"Why do you always do that?" she asked.

"Do what?" Keegan said.

"Act like you're always on. Like the party never stops with you."

Keegan shrugged, eyes on the water. "Why do you always pretend you're made of armor?"

She didn't answer at first.

A gull cried out nearby, soft and strange over the pulse of the music.

"I think I'm gonna hold onto my mask a little longer," Heather said finally. "At least until I figure out what's underneath."

Keegan looked at her—really looked.

"Let me know when you're ready," he said. "I'll do the same."

Behind them, the fire burned steady, its flickering light painting Paige and Dillon in a honey glow.

Paige looked at him, her thoughts spinning. Broad shoulders. Almond-brown eyes. That easy confidence.

God, he was beautiful.

She didn't know him well. Not really. But in that moment, it felt like maybe she didn't need to.

Dillon leaned in, slow and smooth, like the music itself was pulling him forward.

The space between them buzzed—like static, like tension, like the exact second before a kiss becomes real.

Paige's heart pounded. She didn't overthink. She just went for it.

The kiss was quick. Warm. Breathless.

For Dillon, it was an escape.
For Paige, it was everything.

When they broke apart, Dillon offered that familiar, easy grin—like nothing had changed.

But Paige's fingers lingered at her lips, heart stumbling somewhere between the stars and the fire.

The flames crackled softly in front of them, as if secrets still smoldered beneath the ash.

CHAPTER EIGHT — *Reflections*

It was late morning at the Winthrop household, sprinklers twirling across the lawn of the colonial home. The American flag near the front door fluttered in the soft summer breeze.

E.J. knocked lightly on Jane's half-open bedroom door.

"Hey," he called. "Molly's coming over later. We're gonna watch a movie. Wanna join us?"

Jane looked up from her bed, book in hand. "I think I'm good. I'd just be third-wheeling. You and Molly are—whatever you are."

E.J. gave a half-smile. "You wouldn't be third-wheeling. It's just a movie."

Jane shrugged. "You two have fun."

There was a pause. He lingered in the doorway, like he wanted to say more. But he didn't. "Alright. You know where to find us."

When the door clicked shut, Jane exhaled slowly. She rolled up the sleeve of her blouse.

Beneath it, a neutral-toned wrist wrap circled her wrist and palm —tight, discreet, sterile. A quiet reminder of what had happened. Of who she'd started to become.

She remembered the night of Keegan's party—the scream, the mirror, the blood. The desperation to keep her secret from spilling out like the glass.

She pulled the sleeve back down.

At Briarwood Estate, Heather paced in her bedroom wearing silk shorts and a white crop top. On the phone, she continued, "...I have leadership experience, I organized a blood drive and three charity galas—wait, I'm sorry, did you just say minimum wage?"

Her jaw dropped. "Okay, but do I get an assistant at least?"

Click.

She stood frozen, phone still to her ear.

"Hello? Ma'am?"

She threw the phone onto her bed, officially over the job hunt.

Downstairs, chaos had arrived. Voices echoed up the grand staircase—boxes being moved, furniture scraped along marble floors.

Heather crept into the hallway and peeked over the bannister. Two men were bubble-wrapping a chandelier. Folding tables were covered in antiques. Her heart sank.

Her mother, Mrs. Briarwood, swept into the foyer, clipboard in one hand and a half-empty glass of wine in the other.

"What's going on?" Heather asked, hurrying downstairs.

"Liquidation," her mother replied breezily. "Private auction. We're selling what we can to keep the bank at bay."

Heather blinked. "It's starting."

"Start tagging your things, dear."

Heather peeked out the window. The vintage yacht gleamed in the sun like a memory already leaving.

"I was going to throw a surprise party for Paige up there."

Mrs. Briarwood sipped her wine. "Well, surprise! It's being sold."

Down at Raven Lake, Paige and Dillon strolled the dock, ice cream cones in hand. The sun stretched long across the water, casting the town in hues of honey and rose.

"I'm glad you agreed to hang out," Paige said, licking her butter pecan. "There's not much to do around here unless you're into colonial history or clam bakes."

Dillon laughed. "Thanks for inviting me. Honestly, I didn't think I was on your radar."

She smiled. "Even after last night?"

She giggled. "Besides, any guy that treats me to Brady's Ice Cream deserves all the accolades."

They walked in step, passing pastel-painted storefronts with flower boxes and nautical window displays. The air smelled of pine, lakewater, and melted waffle cones.

Dillon glanced over. "Can I ask you something?"

Paige gave a playful gasp. "Of course..."

He hesitated. "Why are you and Heather friends?"

She paused mid-step, then kept walking.

"I'm sorry," he added quickly. "That came out wrong."

Paige let out a soft laugh, though it didn't reach her eyes. "You think I don't fit into her world?"

"No—no, not at all," he said. "It's just... she seems different from you. Kind of intense."

"She can be," Paige admitted. "But Heather's more than she lets on."

Dillon nodded. "I get that. It's just... I heard what she did to that one girl—Molly, I think? You're not like that at all. You don't come across... catty."

Paige went quiet.

After a beat, she spoke, voice softer. "Heather was the first person who really saw me. Even if sometimes I wish she didn't."

She continued, opening up.

"Sometimes I feel like I'm just pretending to belong here. Like everyone else got a manual on how to be perfect, and I'm still learning how to fake it."

She stopped walking.

"I know that sounds dumb."

Dillon shook his head. "It doesn't."

Paige looked out over the lake. The water rippled gently, golden with late afternoon light—calm, quiet, like it was listening.

"I try so hard to act like I don't care what people think, but it's exhausting. You're right about Heather and our differences though, I didn't go to sleepaway camp like these girls or have matching monogrammed towels. My dad's Somali, my mom's Norwegian—I've always been too much of something and never enough of anything. Too Black for the white kids. Too white for the Somali aunties. Too quiet. Too loud. Too smart. Too weird. I can't just be... me."

Her voice cracked. "I don't even know if that's enough."

A tear slid down her cheek.

Dillon stopped beside her. "Paige—"

She wiped her face, laughing bitterly. "God, I'm sorry. I'm a mess."

"You're not." He stepped closer. "You're real. That's what I see when I look at you. Not someone pretending. Someone strong enough to show up as herself."

She looked up at him, eyes glassy, chest tight. "I'm obviously an emotional wreck."

Another tear fell—this time, Dillon wiped it away for her.

"Then wreck here. With me."

She stared at him, trying to understand how a guy like him standing before her, with his good looks, could say all the right things. His voice was soft, steady—not pitying. He meant it.

"No one's ever been this for me," she whispered, lip trembling.

He gently took the dripping cone from her hand and set it on the railing.

"You don't have to hold it all together. Not right now."

Her shoulders gave out first. Then came the sob—sharp, sudden, pulled straight from her chest.

"I hate this town sometimes," she cried, covering her face. "I hate how small it makes me feel. Like I'm always on the outside looking in."

Dillon stepped in, wrapping his arms around her.

She buried her face in his shirt, gripping the fabric like it was the only thing keeping her upright.

"They all act like they have it figured out, like their lives are some perfect picture, and I'm just… blurry in the background."

"I see you, Paige," Dillon murmured. "Clear as day."

She cried harder, letting it all go—the pressure, the pretending, the loneliness no one else noticed.

Dillon just held her.

When her breathing slowed, she pulled back slightly, eyes red, nose running, face blotchy—no walls, no act, just Paige.

"I'm sorry," she sniffed. "You didn't sign up for this."

He hadn't planned on this. On her. But the way she cried—raw and unfiltered—stirred something in him dangerously close to real. Not escape. Not distraction. Something else.

He kissed her softly.

Not to silence her, but to honor her truth. The lake glimmered behind them, like it was holding its breath.

Across town, Sam opened his front door, crutches tucked under his arms.

"Oh, greasy deliverance has arrived."

Maria had arrived to Sam's place holding up a Burger Hut bag, grease already seeping through. "Don't get dramatic. I was craving fries."

"Well, it's a good thing I just happen to be your favorite injured charity case."

They settled into the living room.

"You're not even limping that bad anymore," Maria noted.

Sam smirked. "I'm a warrior."

"That's the spirit," she replied, grabbing a fry and reaching for the remote.

For a moment, it was easy again—sarcasm, salt, and just the two of them.

Then Sam's voice shifted. "Hey… there's something I should tell you."

Maria turned, immediately picking up on the change.

"It's Tyler," he said. "We've been… seeing each other. No one knows. And I kinda want to keep it that way."

Maria didn't blink. "Okay. I can keep it to myself."

Sam nodded, but her expression lingered.

"But?" he asked.

"But it worries me."

He looked down at his lap. "Yeah. I figured."

"You sure this is something you want, Sam?"

"You don't seem surprised."

"I clocked you and Tyler at the party when you ran off."

Sam panicked. "Is it that obvious?"

"Relax. I'm your bestie. I picked up on it, but your secret's safe. I don't think anyone else knows."

He hesitated. "There's a video."

Maria straightened. "What kind of video?"

"The night of Keegan's party. We were in the guesthouse. I thought we were alone. But someone… someone filmed us."

Silence.

Maria sat up straighter. "Sam—if that gets out…"

"I know." He ran a hand over his face. "I've been trying not to spiral. But if someone posts it, or even sends it around—Tyler would lose it. He's not ready for that."

She studied him. "Maybe he should lose it."

Sam looked up, startled. "What?"

"He hurt you, Sam. Physically. He's the reason you're limping around on crutches. And he still gets to kiss you in the dark and pretend you don't exist in daylight?"

"That's not fair—"

"Isn't it?"

Sam shook his head. "You don't know him like I do. It's complicated. Besides, after this, I don't even know if kissing in the dark is a thing anymore."

Maria's voice softened. "I know you. And I hate seeing you scared and still trying to protect the guy who put you in this position."

He looked down again. "If this gets out, it won't just out him. It'll break him. And part of me still… cares."

Maria exhaled. "You're a better person than me."

Sam smiled faintly. "I've always said that."

They both looked down at the bag of fries between them, now cold and forgotten.

Maria nudged it toward him. "Eat. Spiral later."

Night had fallen across Castleton.

In E.J.'s bedroom, Molly curled up beside him, a bowl of popcorn in his lap as a cheesy horror movie played on screen.

Suddenly, the fisherman swung his hook—

Molly screamed. Popcorn flew into the air.

They both burst into laughter, tangled together under the flickering glow of the TV.

"I thought you said this movie was cheesy," she said, brushing kernels off her thigh.

"It is," E.J. grinned. "But hey—there's plenty of fishermen in slickers around Castleton. One might come for you."

She pelted him with popcorn. Their laughter echoed down the hall.

In Jane's room, it was silent.

Her phone buzzed.

She picked it up without thinking.

Unknown Number:
I KNOW YOUR SECRET...

Her chest tightened. The air thinned.

She shot out of bed, suddenly exposed, as if the walls themselves were watching.

She rushed to the window. Empty street. A dog barked somewhere in the distance.

Back in bed, the message burned in her brain. She curled against the wall, heart pounding.

Tate. It had to be Tate. He saw her at Keegan's party. He knows what happened with Johnny.

Had he told someone? Were they talking? Whispering? Heather. Paige. Molly. Dillon. Keegan—
Do they know?

Tears welled up, hot and fast. She fumbled for the orange pill bottle on her nightstand.

Pop. Pills. Swallow.

Her breath hitched in jagged bursts as she pressed her back to the headboard, knees tight to her chest.

Then—

A voice.

Sassy. Familiar. Not hers.

"Oh my god, the waterworks, honey. Give it a rest."

Jane froze.

No one was there.

But the voice echoed, clear and cruel.

She turned toward the mirror.

Her reflection sat on the bed—but it wasn't her.

Jane wore her usual pale blouse, buttoned tight to the neck. Hair pulled back in her classic ponytail.

But the girl in the glass? Loose curls. Black tank top. Red lipstick. A smirk like a blade.

"I'm surprised your tear ducts have any water left. Get a grip, girl."

Jane's lips parted, no words forming.

"Wha-wha-wha… all you do is cry. Cue the violins! It's pathetic. You shouldn't be crying—you should be getting even. And what are you wearing? No wonder we're single."

Jane looked down at her blouse, startled, offended.

"You're not real."

"Oh, I'm very real, Jane. And since you can't handle the heat, maybe it's time you let me take over. I'm the answer to all your problems, girly."

The reflection's smile twisted into something wicked.

CHAPTER NINE- *Too Hot to Handle*

A record-breaking heatwave had settled over Castleton.

At the Castleton Community Pool, the air shimmered with chlorine and sweat, and the concrete steamed beneath bare feet. Kids screamed from the diving boards. Teenagers dripped sunblock and attitude. It was the kind of afternoon where even standing felt like effort.

Girls sprawled on beach towels, glistening in bikinis. Boys lounged shirtless near the edges, flexing without trying too hard. A couple made out under the torn shade of a faded umbrella, legs tangled like vines. Above it all, a tiny speaker buzzed with the town's local radio station.

"It's a scorcher out there, Castleton. Stay hydrated—and try not kill your neighbors. We've got a long summer ahead."

E.J., Molly, and Jane entered through the side gate, immediately hit by the wall of heat and sun.

"I didn't know New England got this hot," Molly said, tugging at her floral tank.

"It's a punishment," E.J. replied.

"For what?" she teased. "Making me watch that slasher last night?"

Jane walked silently beside them, ponytail tight, sunglasses oversized. She wore a cream one-piece and carried herself like she didn't want to be touched by the world.

E.J. peeled off his Castleton High T-shirt, damp with sweat. Molly couldn't help but stare a second too long.

They spotted Maria and Sam already camped beneath a striped umbrella, Sam's crutches propped beside him.

It felt easy. Familiar. The four cousins—plus Molly—falling back into old rhythms.

"We used to run this place," Sam said, twisting the cap off a water bottle. "Saturday swims, Fratelli's pizza, lifeguards threatening to kick us out every other hour."

"I miss that," Maria said. "It felt simpler. Like… before everything."

"We should bring it back," E.J. added. "Cousin days. Feels like we need it."

Molly leaned into him. "Kind of adorable how nostalgic you are."

Jane didn't join the warmth. She sat just outside the circle, reading behind her shades like armor.

"I'm gonna grab water," Molly said, rising. "You good?" she asked E.J., brushing her hand along his knee.

He nodded. "Hydration is survival."

Molly made her way, weaving through the crowd towards the concession stand, past sunbaked kids with popsicles melting faster than they could lick.

She approached the long line of the concession stand, menu above written in chalk. She was still deciding between a raspberry lime rickey or a snow cone when a shadow fell over her.

She turned.

Heather.

Draped in white linen and effortless polish, sunglasses perched in her hair like a crown. "Relax," she said, holding up both hands. "I come in peace."

Heather looked like she had jumped off the pages of an ad for summering in Nantucket.

Molly's jaw tensed. "Didn't expect to see you here."

"There's only one place to be today." Heather offered a faint smile. "I wanted to apologize. No strings. No shade. Just—sorry."

Molly blinked. "You're serious?"

"I've been awful. I know that. I'm not proud of it."

Before Molly could respond, Paige appeared with Dillon, sharing a cherry snow cone, looking blissfully oblivious to the heat. Molly used the moment as a getaway.

Heather's gaze narrowed at the couple. "You two are… attached lately."

"Figured you'd be at Briarwood," Paige replied, unbothered. "Lush gardens, glistening yacht, dipping in your own private pool."

Dillon slipped away, mumbling something about needing a refill.

"I just told Molly—I'm done with the drama," Heather said. "No grudges. Clean slate."

Paige clinked her snow cone against Heather's imaginary glass. "Cheers to your rebrand."

But something in Paige's voice said she wasn't buying the act.

Back at the umbrella, Molly returned empty-handed.

"Where's the drinks?" Sam asked.

"Ran into Heather."

E.J. raised an eyebrow. "She's here?"

Maria groaned. "Slumming it."

"I'd kill for the Briarwood pool right now," Sam added.

"She's a bitch," Jane said flatly behind her glasses. The first thing she'd said all day.

The silence snapped like a rubber band.

Molly stared. Maria blinked. E.J. frowned. Even Sam was caught off guard.

"Jane?" E.J. asked gently.

She didn't answer. Just stood.

"Excuse me," she said. "Need to freshen up."

She disappeared toward the locker rooms. E.J.'s eyes followed, worry beginning to form.

"Well she didn't lie," Sam quipped.

As Jane headed towards the locker room, she caught sight of the parking lot below from the railings.

Keegan's black Range Rover rolled in.

He was shirtless showing off his toned body, shades on, like a moving ad for bad decisions. Heather appeared, climbing into the passenger seat. They laughed. His hand found her thigh.

She didn't move it.

Jane didn't blink.

In the women's locker room, the air was thick with steam and chlorine. Girls passed her in towels, laughing as they dripped toward the diving boards.

Jane passed the mirrors—until one reflection didn't follow.

Jane froze, turning to a mirror. She looked at the glass with her tight ponytail.

In the mirror, her other self leaned casually against the sink, head tilted with a lazy, amused smirk. Hair undone in soft waves, a black bikini top, lip gloss shimmering in red like a threat. Grinning. "Oops. Sorry about that little outburst earlier by the poolside," she said smoothly. "But come on, Heather really is a bitch. Disrespecting our girl Molly? And throwing herself at E.J.? Oh, hell no. She better back the hell back."

Jane's chest tightened.

"Leave me alone," she hissed.

The locker room door creaked open. A woman poked her head in. "Everything alright?"

Jane straightened. "Fine…"

The lady gave a look of worry before shutting the door closed.

Her reflection smirked. "Keep it up and they'll send you to the looney bin."

She stepped closer in the glass.

"And that Keegan we just spotted? Whew. That boy's a snack."

Jane turned away.

"No offense," the reflection added, gesturing at Jane's cream one-piece. "But this look? Discount catalog."

The smile that followed was gleaming, venomous.

"Nighty night, Jane. Time for you to go to sleep for a while."

—

Dusk draped Castleton in molten light.

At the Prescott Estate, Keegan grabbed a jug of water from the fridge. A towel across his shoulder as he stood shirtless chugging it, sweatpants slung low, hair damp from a shower.

An unexpected ring at the front door came.

He made his way lazily to the door, opening it to find…

"Jane?"

But it wasn't Jane.

The girl on the porch was some reimagined version—tank top, cut denim shorts, hair in curls, lips painted crimson. Her confidence hit first.

"You always answer the door half-naked?" she asked, stepping in without waiting.

"You always dress like a video vixen?"

"Only when it counts."

She moved through the foyer, trailing her fingers along the banister.

"Is Heather here?" She asked.

Keegan eyed her.

"No. You here for Heather?" he asked.

She turned. "I'm here for you."

She stepped closer.

He blinked. "You're different."

She reached up, pulled the towel from his shoulder, lips brushing his ear.

"Good different or bad different?"

His hands found her waist before his brain could catch up.

She kissed him on the cheek.

Then eyed him before she went in for the lips.

It was slow. Hot. Dangerous.

And he let her.

Jane liked the game. Hurting Heather without even touching her, while touching him.

He pulled back, breath heavy. "Jane… what's gotten into you?"

"Maybe I'm done pretending."

She stepped in again. "Maybe this is the real me. And you're the only one who gets to see it."

She kissed him again.

Long. Reckless.

He stopped it.

"I can't do this. Jesus, I'm with Heather."

"You can have your cake and eat it too."

"I'm happy with the slice I got."

"Mine tastes better."

He opened the front door. "You should go."

She cocked her head. "Already bored of me?"

"I have something with Heather. I'm not blowing that."

She walked past him, pausing at the door.

"By the way, don't call me Jane."

"What should I call you?"

She smiled, wild and wicked. "DJ."

"What does that stand for?"

"I don't know, maybe Dark Jane…Dangerous Jane. *Delicious Jane*. Or maybe just the Don't-mess-with-me version."

"Dangerous sounds accurate," he said.

She turned, hair flipping over her shoulder.

"There's nothing wrong with a little danger… by the way, next time have an appetite."

She blew him a kiss.

And disappeared into the night.

CHAPTER TEN — *The Weight of Silence*

The morning light filtered through a cracked blind, casting pale lines across a bedroom ruled by discipline. Beneath a faded New England Patriots poster, Tyler James lay flat on his back, tank top clinging to his chest, sweats hanging low on his hips, eyes fixed on the ceiling like he was waiting for judgment. Muscles still tense from yesterday's workout. Mind racing like the scoreboard in the fourth quarter.

Then… pushups.

Palms slapping the hardwood. Veins pulsing in his arms. Grunts sharp. Focus harder. Again. Again. Sweat dripping onto the floorboards like falling seconds on a clock.

Then… he rose.

Pull-ups on the bar wedged into the bathroom doorframe. The frame groaned, but Tyler didn't. Shirtless now. Core tight. He pulls higher, as if he can lift himself out of his body, out of his truth.

This is his morning ritual. Keep the body perfect, keep the mind in line.

The walls around him are lined with proof: trophies, plaques, medals. A mini shrine of effort and expectations.

Knock knock.

He dropped from the bar, chest heaving, just as his father cracked open the door.

"Bible study tonight," his father said. "Be home on time."

"Okay," Tyler replied, already reaching for a towel.

He was raised on obedience. Faith before feeling. A prayer at every meal. Baptism photos still framed in the hallway.

He remembered the cold weight of the priest's hand, the water closing over him. A clean slate, they said. Washed of sin. Born again. He wished he'd stayed under, drowned right then and there— but then... resurfacing , shivering, water sliding off his head as a new man.

Coming back to reality, Tyler entered his bathroom, looking at his reflection while brushing his teeth. Swish. Spit. Floss. He watches his jaw work. His eyes stay cold.

His mother's voice echoed in his mind.

When are you going to bring a nice girl home, Ty?

He tried. He remembers the girl from school—Courtney? Caitlyn? The blonde one. They had sex once. She called it perfect. He called it cardio. He even brought her home to dinner once. Laugh at the right places. Kiss her on the cheek when his mom looked over.

Then he dumped her.

He tried to do it kindly. Thought he was being mature. But she cried—really cried. And he just stood there. Dry-eyed. Empty.

He didn't feel bad. He felt free.

Then, the memory that always comes back when he least expects it: the locker room. Steam curling off the tiled floor. Post-practice exhaustion. The sting of hot water on sore shoulders.

Only Gabe was left in the shower with him. Tall, sculpted, naked. Tyler looked.

And he liked what he saw, his gaze lingering... then his body started to respond.

He turned quickly, his back to Gabe—pretended to adjust the temperature of his water. Heart hammering louder than the water hitting the tile.

But now in the present, as he stared at himself in the mirror. He felt broken.

He really liked Sam. A lot. Sam makes him feel seen… alive. What started as a casual hookup from an app had turned real.

But it could never be he thought.

Coming out to his family would be an exorcism.
Coming out to the football team? A crucifixion.

And now Dillon has the video.

It's just a matter of time.

Before the shoe drops.

Before everything does.

Tyler clenches his fist.

BAM.

He drives it through the wall beside his dresser. Plaster cracks. Blood blooms across his knuckles.

The hole stares back at him—wide and gaping, like the life he's been trying to hide.

Across town, Dillon's phone—*that* phone—lay screen-down on the couch. Silent. Still.

Dillon stood at his front door as Paige arrived, smile easy, shoulders relaxed, her presence like a window cracked open on a too-warm day.

"Hey, I missed you," she said, stepping in.

Dillon smiled, soft and automatic. "Someone's birthday is coming up, huh?"

"You remembered."

They laughed as they settled on the couch. But Dillon's pulse didn't match his smile.

"I need to tell you something," he said finally, voice quieter than usual. "And I need you to really hear me."

Paige's smile faded, but not her warmth. "You can tell me anything."

Dillon reached for his laptop. He hesitated.

"I recorded something at Keegan's party on my phone. It wasn't on purpose. I was just messing around and…" He clicked. A video loaded.

Paige leaned in, her brow furrowed.

"I uploaded it here on my laptop. It's Tyler," Dillon said. "And Sam. They were in the guesthouse. It started with a kiss."

His hand trembled on the trackpad. Once he hit play, there'd be no pretending he didn't know.

Then-

He hit it.

The kiss. The fall. The crash.

Paige froze.

Dillon's voice dropped. "Tyler shoved him. Sam hit the table. That's how he ended up in the hospital."

Paige stared at the screen, eyes wide. "Jesus."

"I don't know what to do," Dillon admitted. "I haven't shown anyone. Not even Sam. But I know what I saw."

"Do you think Tyler meant to hurt him?"

Dillon shook his head. "I think Tyler panicked. But that doesn't make it okay."

Paige didn't answer right away. She took his hand.

"If that video gets out," she said carefully, "it could ruin Tyler. But it might also protect Sam."

"I know."

"And if you delete it…"

Dillon sighed. "Then no one knows what really happened."

They sat in the silence, the weight of it pressing down.

Finally, Paige said, "You have to decide what matters more: protecting someone who's afraid, or standing up for someone who got hurt."

Dillon closed the laptop.

That night, after Bible study, Tyler came home.

The house was still. He unbuttoned his shirt, moved to the edge of his bed. Same trophies. Same cracked wall. Nothing had changed, and everything had.

He picked up his phone.

SAM was still pinned to the top of his contacts.

He typed: *I miss you.*

Stared. Deleted.

Then typed it again.

And hit **send**.

On the other side of town, Sam sat on the couch, blanket over his lap. Maria was asleep beside him, her breathing soft, the TV flickering low in the background.

His phone buzzed.

Tyler: I miss you.

Sam stared.

He typed: *I miss you too.*

He meant it with everything. Then he paused, glancing over at Maria.

Then—*Delete.*

He buried the phone beneath the blanket, eyes tearing.

The fan overhead whirred. The TV whispered. And Sam sat motionless, his heart knocking against his ribs like it wanted out.

In two separate houses, two boys stared at nothing, feeling everything.

And no one said a word.

CHAPTER ELEVEN — *Unraveling*

The afternoon sun spilled hot and golden across Dillon's backyard. He stood on a chair, looping strands of string lights along the patio rafters, while Keegan arranged plastic cups into perfect pyramids.

"You're really going all out for Paige," Keegan said, nodding toward the balloons swaying lazily in the heat and the cake box perched on a cooler. "Didn't know you were the party-planning type."

Dillon smirked as he stepped down to unknot a strand. "Wasn't supposed to be all this."

Keegan raised a brow. "Meaning...?"

"Meaning it started as a distraction," Dillon admitted. "Life got too hot, too fast. Paige was... there. No games, no chaos. Just chill." He paused. "And then she turned out to be kind of perfect. Lucky I got her."

Keegan laughed. "And Erica's just cool with that?"

Dillon scoffed. "Erica? That girl's a hurricane. One minute she's jealous if I breathe near someone else, next she ghosts like I never existed. I couldn't keep up."

"Yeah, she's intense," Keegan said, leaning against the shed. "But Paige? She's real, I dig her."

Then he hesitated, thumb brushing the edge of a solo cup. "Heather sees me."

Dillon looked over. "What's that supposed to mean?"

Keegan shrugged. "It's not just about looks. Heather picks up on things I don't even say. It freaks me out sometimes... but I don't want to mess that up. She gets me."

There was a pause before Keegan added, quieter, "But last night... Jane came on to me."

Dillon blinked. "Wait—Jane Winthrop?"

Keegan nodded. "Except... it didn't feel like Jane. Different energy. Different look. Bolder. Like she'd been switched out for someone else entirely."

Dillon raised an eyebrow. "You sure you weren't just drunk?"

Keegan shook his head. "No. It was her—but not her. Like she stepped out of her own skin."

A couple blocks away, Heather stood in front of Paige's open closet, manicured fingers flicking through hangers. "Okay, honest question... is this it?"

Paige sat cross-legged on the bed, eyebrows lifting. "Yup. Unless you count what's in the laundry basket."

Heather pulled out a plain navy sundress, holding it in front of herself with the delicacy of someone handling an antique. "This is cute. Very... humble."

Paige laughed lightly, but there was tension underneath. "Heather."

"I didn't mean it like that," Heather backpedaled. "I just... I'm used to more variety. But hey—thrift store chic is having a moment."

Paige's smile didn't quite reach her eyes. "Good to know I'm trendy by accident. You know what, I'm fine with what I'm wearing now."

The silence stretched.

Heather softened. "What you're wearing now looks good. Really. It's... you."

Paige glanced down—cutoffs, a worn tank, old sneakers. It was exactly her. And that's what made it sting.

"You don't have to lie."

"I'm not," Heather said, voice quieter. "Sometimes... I feel that too. Like whatever I put on, it's still not enough. Not really."

Paige looked up, startled by the honesty. For a moment, Heather wasn't armor and lip gloss—just a girl.

"You make simple look cool," Heather added, almost begrudgingly. "It's kind of infuriating."

A reluctant laugh slipped from Paige. "Well... I try."

Heather stepped closer, fixing a twisted strap on Paige's top, fingers brushing her shoulder—so lightly it didn't feel accidental.

"You sure this outfit's okay for where we're going?" Paige asked. "Just tell me."

Heather smirked. "If I told you, it wouldn't be a surprise, now would it?"

"Not even a hint?"

"Nope." She reached for Paige's hand. "C'mon. The day waits for no one."

In the Lockhart backyard, the sun stretched long across the lawn, casting gold light over the grass and hedges. The air was warm but softening, evening drifting in slow.

Mr. Lockhart stood half-submerged in the garden shed, shifting through boxes and tangled cords with increasing frustration. From inside came the sound of muttering and the occasional thump as he searched for something he'd misplaced.

E.J. and Molly lounged on the cushioned patio loveseat, sunk deep into each other. Molly's knees were tucked up, E.J.'s arm draped over her shoulders. One of his fingers absentmindedly traced a lazy circle across her arm while her cheek leaned into his chest.

"Are you sure he's okay in there?" E.J. asked, glancing toward the shed as something metal clattered loudly to the ground.

Molly grinned against him. "He says he's looking for the ratchet set. But honestly, I think he just wants an excuse to reorganize everything and complain while doing it."

A low curse floated out from the shed.

E.J. chuckled. "I feel like I should offer to help."

"He'll say no," Molly said, curling tighter into his side.

They both laughed, that easy kind of laughter that only comes when there's no rush to be anywhere else. E.J. kissed the top of her head softly and rested his cheek against her hair.

The shed door creaked again as Mr. Lockhart reappeared, holding a wrench triumphantly in one hand and wiping sweat from his brow with the other.

He looked over at the loveseat, taking in the sight of them cuddling in the golden hour light.

"You've made Molly's transition here a lot easier," he said, his voice gruff but gentle. "You're a good man, E.J."

E.J. sat up a little straighter, startled but grateful. "Thank you, sir."

Mr. Lockhart gave a small nod, then disappeared back into the shed with the air of someone who'd said exactly what he meant.

Then—

"E.J.!"

They both turned.

Jane leaned casually over the picket fence from the Winthrop side —sunglasses low, curls bouncing, her crop top just shy of scandalous. She looked... lit from within. Different. With a smirk and confidence dialed up, her energy was sharp in a way that made Molly instinctively sit up.

And just like that, the quiet shifted.

E.J. made his way over.

"You and Molly wanna come to Paige's surprise party tonight?" she asked, voice breezy.

E.J. raised an eyebrow. "Since when are you and Paige tight?"

Jane shrugged. "We're not. I just feel like dancing."

Something in her tone made him pause—like a tremor under the surface.

"I was planning on hanging with Molly tonight," he said.

Jane's smile faltered. "Fine. I'll text Sam. At least he knows how to have fun."

She adjusted her sunglasses and turned away.

E.J. stood frozen for a beat before returning to the patio, brow furrowed.

"She's off," he said. "Since Harmony she's been quiet, reserved. This new her is… jarring."

"What happened in Harmony?" she asked gently.

E.J. looked down. His voice was almost a whisper. "I let her down."

Minutes later, a red Honda Civic pulled up in front of the Winthrop home.

Jane walked down the driveway like she owned it, now in heels clicking, a red sequin mini dress catching the sun. She tossed her purse into the back seat and climbed in.

"Hello, cousins," she purred.

Sam grinned in the mirror. "Hello, legs."

"You're on aux," Maria added, eyeing Jane's look. "What are we listening to, DJ?"

Jane's grin widened. "DJ. I like that."

She scrolled Sam's phone with purpose. "This one."

A$AP Ferg's "Plain Jane" blasted from the speakers. The bass shook the windows.

"Sunroof," she ordered.

Sam hit the switch. Jane climbed up and out, standing, wind catching her curls as she shouted lyrics to the sky.

Maria blinked. "Okay... that's new."

"She's on another level tonight," Sam said, laughing.

Behind them, the sun dipped toward the treetops, painting the sky in streaks of gold and rose. And still, under the music and movement and laughter, something else pulsed— unseen, but rising.

CHAPTER TWELVE — *Under the Lights*

The sun dipped low over Castleton, streaking the rooftops in gold. Most homes had gone still for the evening, but Dillon's backyard hummed with soft music and laughter. String lights twinkled from the trees, and the scent of barbecue drifted through the air. No strobe lights or smoke machines. Just warmth, friends, and a heartbeat kind of joy.

Keegan leaned on the fence, eyeing the setup with a crooked grin. "Not bad, party planner."

Dillon adjusted a speaker near the porch, then gave him a half-smile.

"It's not a Keegan-level blowout, but it works."

Keegan chuckled. "Lowkey's underrated, it might be the move for my eighteenth next month."

"Yeah, right," said Dillon, his eyes turning toward the driveway. Any minute now.

Gravel crunched underfoot as Paige followed Heather up the path, the air thick with cut grass and possibility.

Then—

"Surprise!"

Voices erupted in cheers. String lights blinked above. Paige froze, wide-eyed, as a burst of confetti showered her. Up on the porch, Dillon held the empty cannon like a bouquet.

For a beat, she just stood there.

Then he was already descending the stairs, wrapping his arms around her and kissing her like he meant it.

"You did all this?" she breathed.

"Happy birthday," he said, grinning.

She let him lead her into the glow of the yard.

Three more figures stepped into the party: Sam—walking without crutches, though careful. Maria beside him. And behind them, Jane.

Red sequins. Heels. Hair wild. She stepped inside like a loaded gun with glitter on the grip.

Her eyes scanned the yard like searchlights. She wasn't looking for friends. She was looking for him… Keegan.

The music slowed. Laughter softened. Couples found each other.

Dillon pulled Paige close, arms slipping around her waist.

"I should've worn something else," she murmured.

He brushed a strand of hair from her cheek.

"You look like you. That's the point."

She tried to smile. "I just… don't feel like I belong."

"You do," he said gently. "You do with me."

She kissed his cheek and pulled away.

"I'm gonna grab a drink."

He let her go. But something in him tightened.

At the cooler, Paige searched for a drink, then eyed the tequila bottle on the table. She grabbed it and took a swig.

"You okay?" Heather asked, approaching.

"I'm fine."

"You know you're a lightweight."

"Maybe I've built tolerance," Paige said, sipping and walking off.

Heather watched her walk away, concern flickering behind her lashes.

Near the gate, Keegan nudged Dillon.

"She's here."

"Who—" Dillon turned. And saw her.

Erica… Cool. Beautiful. Uninvited.

Dillon cut through the yard, approaching her.
"You weren't invited."

She shrugged. "Didn't think I needed an invitation."

"You need to leave."

"I will. Right after I say happy birthday to the girl who got my leftovers."

His jaw clenched. He grabbed her arm and steered her inside.

Inside the house, Paige wandered down a hallway towards the bathroom, swigging the last bit of alcohol from the bottle empty. She just wanted a second. A breather.

As she neared the bathroom—

Laughter. Voices.

"She didn't even try."
"What is she wearing?"
"She's a placeholder."
"Dillon could do way better."

Paige froze.

Then backed away. Found the nearest door. Opened it.

A closet.

She stepped inside, closed it behind her, and sank to the floor.

Knees to chest. Breaths shallow. Darkness wrapping around her like a blanket she hadn't asked for.

Outside the closet door: music and footsteps.
 Inside: stillness.

Then—

"I love your dress, Jane," someone said exiting the bathroom. "So chic," the other girl added.

Jane: "Thanks, cuties. The birthday girl could've used it."

Laughter. Cruel and easy.

Paige pressed her back into the wall. Bit her lip.

And the tears came—hot, quiet, and slow.

CHAPTER THIRTEEN — *Betrayal*

The music pulsed on outside, low and rhythmic, but inside the closet, it was suffocating.

Paige sat curled on the floor, arms wrapped tight around her knees, mascara smudged and throat raw. The bass thumped like a second heartbeat, distant and cruel. Her cheek pressed to the wall, cold and grounding, but it wasn't enough to stop the shivering.

The empty alcohol bottle sat beside her.

I shouldn't have come, she thought.

Light flickered beneath the closet door. Footsteps passed. Laughter. Then silence.

In that silence, something cracked. A shift. She could stay in here —let shame devour her, let humiliation root itself deep. Or… she could move.

She braced a hand on the wall and stood, wavering. The tequila still pulsed through her bloodstream—warm and disorienting—but something else surged now too: instinct.

She opened the door.

The hallway blurred before her, walls breathing in and out. She needed Dillon. Just to see him. Just to remember she wasn't completely alone.

She staggered forward, leaving behind the version of herself who'd smiled when the confetti fell.

In Dillon's room, Erica sat cross-legged on the edge of his bed, calm like a viper before it strikes.

"So," she said, voice like honey edged in venom, "why didn't I know about Paige?"

Dillon exhaled, tired. "We're not together anymore. I don't owe you an explanation."

Her expression didn't change. "I always figured we'd get back together."

"We won't." His tone sharpened. "You're toxic."

Erica stood, her lips curving into something between a pout and a smirk. "That's mean," she said, stepping in too close. "But not wrong."

Dillon backed up. "Erica—"

He didn't hear the door open behind him, muffled by the music.

Paige froze in the doorway.

The room tilted slightly. Her breath hitched.

Erica had seen her.

And with the slow, practiced cruelty of someone who knew exactly where to drive the knife, Erica leaned in—and kissed Dillon.

Time splintered.

Paige's heart cracked. Her vision blurred. The sob hit her like a gut punch—deep and silent, shaking her from the inside out.

She turned away just as Dillon pulled back, a second too late.

"What the hell is wrong with you?" he snapped, then noticing his bedroom door was wide open.

"Anyone could've seen—"

Erica smiled. "Guess you didn't close the door tight enough."

"Get out," he growled.

She rolled her eyes. "With pleasure."

But the damage was already done.

Paige stumbled into the living room. The floor swam beneath her. Her stomach lurched.

And then—she vomited. Right there, onto the hardwood. The sound was louder in her soul than the music ever could be.

She wiped her mouth with the back of her hand, trembling.

She flopped onto the couch. The same couch she and Dillon had once sat on when things were soft. Hopeful.

And then—Dillon's laptop. Sitting. Waiting.

The memory of the video snapped into focus.

That folder. The file.

She tried to bury the bathroom voices, but they echoed louder now, meaner, sharper.

"She didn't even try."
"What is she wearing?"
"She's a placeholder."
"Dillon could do way better."

And then the moment that hurt her the most flashed into her mind— Erica standing there kissing Dillon, the one person she thought she could trust. Erica's gaze burning through her soul.

Paige began breathing heavy from the thought. Her eyes refocusing on the laptop again.

He had shown her once. Trusted her. She had sworn to protect it.

But promises were for people who mattered.

He gets to humiliate me and still be the good guy? No. Not this time, she thought.

Her hands fumbled to open the laptop, then her fingers hovered over the trackpad. Her reflection stared back in the screen—red-eyed, broken.

Her hands moved without permission. Her mind screamed stop, but her body had already betrayed her—just like everyone else had.

Don't do it, something inside whispered.

But she clicked anyway.

The video posted.

Her hand flew to her mouth as she jumped, immediate regret setting in as her phone slipped from her lap and hit the floor.

She scrambled after it, heart pounding.

Buzz.

A new notification.

Dillon Powell just posted a video.

The front door stretched before her, impossibly far. She could still run through it.

Outside, the party had thinned. Maria stood by the patio steps. Sam approached, cup in hand.

"Seen Jane?" she asked.

"She's getting her own ride," Sam said.

Maria's phone buzzed. She looked.

And froze.

Sam leaned over. "What is it?"

He watched from over her shoulder.

The kiss. The crash. His own body slamming into a table.

His breath caught. A chill ran down his back.

"Oh God— Tyler."

Across the yard, Heather and Keegan were watching the same video. Heather's stomach turned. The crash in the video made her turn her head, she couldn't watch another moment of it. She quickly changed the subject.

"Paige is missing," she said, already moving.

"I'll come—"

"No." THeather said, then softer. "Stay. Help Dillon clean up."

Keegan nodded slowly. "You okay?"

"I will be," Heather said. "Once I find her."

The yard was nearly empty now. Keegan grabbed a beer bottle from the cooler and snapped it open.

Behind him, a shadow shifted across the fence.

He turned.

Jane.

"Jane…" he said, startled.

"Come with me," she said softly.

She grabbed his hand, leading him to the shed.

The door creaked open. The single light flicked on above, dangling. Tools, fertilizer, and a chair meticulously place in the center of it all.

Keegan stepped in. "What is this?"

"I've been wanting to get you alone all night," she said, locking the door behind her.

He gave a breathy laugh. "You're trouble."

"I prefer unpredictable."

She gestured for him to sit. He hesitated, then dropped into the chair, beer bottle in hand.

She circled behind him.

"I told you—I'm with Heather," he said.

"Heather's not here."

Her hands slid to his shoulders. He tensed.

"This isn't right," he muttered.

Her fingers pressed into a knot on his back, she massaged it out, his body betraying him by loosening up.

But his mind still fought. He turned slightly to look at her.

"Jane... seriously."

"Don't call me Jane," she said as she circled back in front of him, straddling him now. "Just let go."

She kissed him.

He resisted, briefly. One of his hands caught her wrist—then she grabbed the beer from his other hand taking a swig. He grabbed it back, finishing it.

"I hope you brought that appetite I told you to bring."

The beer bottle clinked to the floor. Her fingers unfastened his belt.

He didn't stop her.

One last breath of hesitation. A flash of Heather's laugh in his mind.

Gone.

His shirt hit the floor, then she stood, guided his hand to the back zipper of her dress. He slid it down every curve exploring her body.

That night, in the heat of the shed—

Keegan gave in.

CHAPTER FOURTEEN— *Damage is Done*

Despite the clouds, morning light spilled into Jane's bedroom—soft and gold. It brushed against tangled sheets and kissed her bare legs as she lay sprawled in an oversized T-shirt, curls wild around her head like a halo snapped out of place.

She was already awake.

A giggle slipped from her lips—girlish and giddy.

She'd scored Keegan last night.

The memory shimmered like heat behind her eyes.

"I can't wait for Heather to find out," she whispered to the ceiling, smile curling. "Queen Bee, dethroned."

She laughed again—sharper now. Almost wicked, kicking her legs into the air.

"Stop it."

The voice was hers. But not.

Her eyes snapped to the mirror. Her reflection stared back—except it wasn't her. Not quite. The girl in the glass wore her face, but it had been tightened, smoothed, restrained. A neat ponytail. A buttoned blouse. Lips tight. Eyes hurt.

"What the hell?" Jane muttered.

The reflection didn't blink. "What have you done?"

Jane scoffed. "Relax. We had fun. Isn't that what you always wanted?"

"No," the reflection said. Voice trembling. "You need to let me back in. This isn't who we are."

Jane stood, pulse quick, something manic in her limbs.

"No," she whispered. "This is the real me. You were just too scared to set it free."

They stared at each other—fractured versions caught in opposing glass.

Then—

Knock knock.

E.J.'s voice came from the other side of the door. "Jane?"

She cracked open the door. He stood there in joggers and a tank, blinking away sleep.

"How was the party?"

Jane smiled, almost devilish. "Perfect. A night to remember."

He studied her face. Something felt off. Off in a way he couldn't name.

"Cool. Well… camp planning later, don't flake."

"Sure," she said, easing the door shut.

Then she turned to the bed and collapsed onto it like a queen collapsing into velvet.

"Let them pitch tents," she murmured. "I've got bigger things in store."

Raven Lake was swallowed in fog, morning mist curling off the glassy surface like breath on cold glass.

Sam stood at the edge in silence, hoodie sleeves pulled over his hands. He hadn't slept.

Behind him, soft footsteps.

"Sam."

He turned. Tyler appeared like a ghost, hood up, eyes hollow.

"You saw it?" Tyler asked.

Sam nodded. "Everyone did."

Tyler exhaled. "It's already viral. Texts. DMs. Bible quotes. Laughter." His voice cracked. "My parents haven't seen it yet... but they will."

They walked in silence down the trail, fog snaking around their feet like something alive.

"Why would Dillon do that?" Sam asked finally.

Tyler shook his head. "Doesn't matter. The damage is done."

Sam stopped. "I never replied," he said quietly. "To your text the other night. When you said you missed me."

Tyler looked at him.

"I miss you too," Sam said. "So much. I was just scared. Hiding felt safer than actually losing you."

Sam stepped closer.

"If there was a world where we could just be… I'd want that. More than anything."

Tyler's voice was barely audible. "I hurt you."

"You've apologized. And I meant it when I forgave you."

"But I don't trust myself not to become that guy again."

"You're not him," Sam whispered.

And then—he kissed him. Slow. Gentle. Sure.

"I love you," Sam said.

"I love you too," Tyler replied, without hesitation.

They held each other as Raven Lake rippled behind them, the fog rising like it was trying to protect something sacred.

At Briarwood Estate, the fog drifted like smoke across the grounds.

Inside, Paige sat in Heather's bed, knees drawn to her chest, staring out the tall windows toward town.

"I can't believe I sent the video," she said softly.

Heather stirred beside her. "Are you even sure what you saw?"

"I thought I saw them kiss. Erica and Dillon. But I was so upset. Drunk. I don't know."

Heather sat up, propped against a pillow. "That sounds like most girls here on a Friday."

Paige half-laughed. "I ruined everything."

"You were hurt," Heather said. "It doesn't excuse it, but… I've been there."

Paige checked her phone. Missed calls from Dillon. Her stomach dropped.

"Thanks for letting me stay."

"You were a wreck," Heather said plainly. "I wasn't gonna let you unravel alone."

Heather gave Paige a reassuring look. She meant what she said.

Paige needed to hear that. "Thank you."

Heather brushed a stray hair out of Paige's face, staring at her a little too close, as Paige addressed the elephant in the room… or lack thereof.

"Where's all your stuff?" Paige asked.

"Briarwood's going on the market."

"What?"

Heather reached for her untouched Fiji water. "You must've missed the for sale sign when you stumbled in last night. We're broke. If I don't get a job soon, my mother's literally going to kill me. The vibe's very apocalyptic."

Paige blinked. "Heather… I didn't know."

Heather smirked, but it didn't touch her eyes. "It's just Castleton, babe. This town breaks everyone eventually."

Paige turned back toward the window. "What do we even do now?"

Heather didn't hesitate. "Well for you, first step is to talk to Dillon…"

Down at the docks, Dillon ran hard, trying to outrun everything.

He never saw Tyler coming.

Tyler jumped and tackled him mid-stride. Dillon hit the dock with a thud. His earbuds flew. His phone skidded across the planks— and disappeared into the lake with a splash.

"What the hell!?"

"You posted the video!" Tyler shouted.

"I didn't!" Dillon gasped, shoving him off. "I swear to God!"

"You're the only one who had it!"

They tumbled, fists flailing, rage overflowing. Until Dillon stumbled backwards—

SPLASH!

The lake swallowed him whole.

He surfaced seconds later, sputtering, soaked, eyes wild.

"I didn't do it!" Dillon yelled from the water.

Tyler stood at the edge of the dock, in fury.

"Then someone you trusted did," Tyler said. "And I'm the one bleeding for it."

He turned and walked away.

Dillon stayed there—floating, shivering—while the sky pressed down, and Castleton, once again, swallowed someone whole.

CHAPTER FIFTEEN— *Just Existing*

Paige remembered her first week at Castleton High like it had been etched into her bones.

Freshman year. New town. New building. Same ache of not quite belonging.

The hallway lights buzzed overhead as she moved past lockers, hugging her books to her chest like armor. Every step felt scanned, judged. Even the Hellcat mascot above the main entrance seemed to leer down at her like it knew she didn't belong, ready to claw.

To her left: a pack of varsity boys. One bit into an apple and gave her a slow once-over like she was the next thing on the menu.

To her right: the popular girls leaned against lockers like models in a catalog. Heather among them. All precision smiles and silent calculation.

In the cafeteria, it didn't get better.

"This seat's taken," a girl said without looking up.

Paige turned. The nerd table looked open. But that label stuck fast —and she couldn't afford another layer of exclusion.

So she sat alone. Not quite loner, not quite lost. Just… nothing.

Then came science class. Frog dissection day.

Her lab partner—a boy in a faded band hoodie that reeked of Axe —tilted his head at her.

"What… are you?"

She blinked. "Me or the frog?"

He smirked. "Like… are you Black? Or… mixed or something?"

"I'm a person," she said flatly. "Focus."

They looked down at the frog. It reeked of formaldehyde and something quieter—resentment.

She wasn't first-picked. She wasn't last. She just… existed.

One day in class, the teacher announced a field trip to New York City. Everyone buzzed with excitement.

That night at home, Paige asked her mom—a tired woman with Nordic features, worn hands and eyes that stayed on the bills even as Paige spoke.

"I can't afford that," her mom said. "You want groceries this week, or a bus ride to Manhattan?"

So: no field trip. No photos. No memory made. Just more of the same.

Until gym class.

Heather strolled up in her Hellcats uniform like she owned the gym and everyone in it. Her posse not far behind.

"You're cute," she said, arms crossed.

Paige blinked. "Thanks… but I don't swing that way."

Heather laughed. Loud. "Not like that. I mean you've got the look. You ever thought about cheer?"

Cheerleading?

Paige thought of her off-brand sneakers in a sea of Nikes. Her mom's car barely making it up the hill to school. Did Heather even realize how different their lives were?

Apparently not.

But Paige said yes.

And after that, she had a spot. Not quite Heather's equal—but close. A seat at the table. A title. An identity, even if it meant a shadow.

So when Heather told her to talk to Dillon, it wasn't just advice. It was a challenge.

Paige stood now on Dillon's porch, heart pounding. The sidewalk still held mist from the morning rain, damp and clinging.

She knocked.

Dillon's dad answered. "Hey, Paige."

"Is he home?" she asked.

Mr. Powell shook his head. "He went out. Want me to tell him you stopped by?"

She hesitated. "No… that's okay."

But it wasn't. Not really. It was delaying the inevitable.

Across town, the sun was bruising the sky as it began to set.

Outside The Burger Hut, Erica and her friends walked out laughing, grease-stained leftovers in bags.

Dillon stood near the curb, hoodie up, a bruise forming under one eye.

"Erica," he called.

She stopped. Her friends quieted.

"Give me a sec," she told the girls, stepping forward. "Damn. What happened to you?"

Dillon's jaw clenched. "Where's Paige?"

Erica blinked. "How should I know?"

"Did you tell her something? After the party? Did you mess with her?"

Erica narrowed her eyes. "Why would I?"

"I don't know! But she's ignoring me—and I'm not gonna let you screw with her head."

Paige stepped around the corner just in time to hear the commotion. She'd been on her way home, drawn by the voices. She froze when she saw them.

"I know what you did," Dillon said.

Erica scoffed. "You're seriously delusional."

"You tried to manipulate her. And you forced yourself on me."

Paige's eyes widened.

"What did you just say?" Erica snapped.

Dillon's voice cracked. "You touched me. When I said no, and I know you sent that video from my laptop."

"You're out of your mind."

"You're not gonna gaslight me out of this," he said, shaking. "You crossed a line."

Erica's gaze shifted and landed on Paige.

"He's all yours," she muttered, then stormed off.

Dillon turned—saw Paige—and for a second, his face softened.

"She sent the video," he said quietly. "I can't believe it."

"I did," Paige said.

He blinked.

"What?"

"I sent it," she repeated. "It wasn't her. It was me."

The air seemed to stop.

He stepped back, shaking his head. "No. No, why would you do that?"

"I was drunk—I was confused—I saw you with Erica and—"

"You didn't even ask," he cut in. "You didn't even talk to me."

"I know," she said, tears welling. "I'm sorry. I swear, I didn't mean to—"

"I can't even look at you," he said, voice cracking. "Not right now."

He turned.

She flinched as he walked past her—fast, furious, leaving her behind.

A ceramic planter sat near the Burger Hut entrance. Dillon stopped, grabbed it, and hurled it against the brick wall.

It shattered. Soil exploded across the sidewalk.

She didn't flinch. Maybe because something inside her had already shattered first.

That night, across town, another fallout was beginning.

Tyler unlocked the door to his house and stepped inside, heading upstairs.

Then—

"Tyler."

He froze.

His father stood at the foot of the stairs.

"We need to talk." Mr. James said, voice low, quiet.

But deadly sharp.

CHAPTER SIXTEEN— *Let the Rain Fall Down*

"Tyler."

His father's voice stopped him cold at the base of the stairs.

Mr. James stood there—arms crossed, face unreadable—but the air between them was sharp with fury.

"We need to talk." His voice was low. Clipped.

Tyler's hand tightened on the banister. He didn't answer.

"Look at me."

Tyler turned slowly.

"I didn't raise no faggot."

Tyler flinched. "What are you talking about, Dad—?"

"Save it." His father's voice sliced through him. "The whole church is talking. That video's out. I've seen it—on phones, on Facebook. It's everywhere."

Tyler already knew. He'd seen the comments, the reposts, the private messages. Still, hearing it from his father didn't sting the same —it shattered something deeper.

His eyes burned.

"Don't cry," his father snapped. "Pull yourself together. You've gone astray. Chosen this perverted lifestyle."

His voice rose.

"Your mother and I raised you better than this. What kind of example are you to your little sister?"

Footsteps behind them.

Mrs. James stepped in from the kitchen, towel in hand.

"What is all this yelling?"

Mr. James didn't look at her. "Your son says he's gay."

She stopped mid-step, staring. Something behind her eyes cracked.

"Jesus," Tyler muttered. "Does it matter that much?"

"Yes, it matters!" she barked. "I will not stand by while my son buys a one-way ticket to hell!"

Tyler snapped. "Oh my God—"

He spun and bolted up the stairs. His bedroom door slammed behind him.

But Mr. James wasn't finished.

The door burst open a second later. He grabbed Tyler by the arm.

"Do I need to shake some sense into you?"

"Get off me!" Tyler shoved him back, breath ragged.

"You hear me? The devil is chasing you now. I won't have that filth in my house. You need to get out."

"And go where?!"

"Anywhere but here."

A long pause.

Tyler's fists trembled. His father stepped in again—too close.

This time, Tyler shoved him—hard—into the doorframe.

Mrs. James appeared in the hallway, frozen.

"Get out!" Mr. James roared.

"Fine!" Tyler grabbed a duffel bag from under the bed, yanked open drawers. Jeans. Hoodies. Whatever his hands could find.

He shouldered the bag and stormed past them, bumping into his father one last time on the way out.

Neither parent followed.

That night, Castleton exhaled in rain.

At Briarwood, Heather's once-grand bedroom was nearly bare. The walls stripped. Her vanity gone. No pink neon glow. Just silence.

Paige sobbed into Heather's shoulder, wrecked and unraveling. Heather said nothing. Just held her. Stroked her hair slow and steady.

She stayed.

Outside the Burger Hut, Dillon sat in his car, rain streaking the windshield in long, silver threads. His fists clenched against the steering wheel.

He hadn't moved since Paige left.

Three breaths. Then he slammed his fists—once, twice—against the dash. The sound cracked through the stillness.

Then—movement.

Through the glass, a figure emerged.

Tyler.

Drenched. A duffel bag slung over his shoulder. Head down. Nowhere to go.

Dillon blinked.

He turned on the headlights. Eased the car forward. Pulled up beside him.

Rolled down the window.

"Hey, Ty."

Tyler looked up. Saw him.

And ran.

"Ty—"

Dillon threw the car into park and bolted out into the rain. "Tyler, wait!"

He caught up, grabbed his shoulder—gently, just enough to stop him.

"Get off me!" Tyler spun, fists up.

Dillon backed off, hands raised. "Okay—okay. I'm not trying to hurt you."

Tyler's breath came fast. Rain dripped from his hood. Jaw clenched.

"Then why the hell are you chasing me?"

"You ran."

"No shit."

A beat. Just rain between them.

"What do you want?" Tyler asked, voice rough.

"I didn't post that video," Dillon said. "It was Paige."

Tyler blinked. "What?"

"She was drunk. Upset. I'm not saying it's okay, but… she lost it."

Tyler looked away. "That makes two of us."

Dillon's eyes dropped to the bag. "They kicked you out?"

Tyler didn't answer.

He didn't have to.

Dillon nodded. "You can crash at my place."

Tyler stared at him. "Why would you even want to help me?"

"You think I'm gonna let you wander Castleton with a bag in the rain?"

"You're the reason I need the damn bag!"

"I know," Dillon said softly. "But still."

He moved to the car. Opened the passenger door.

"Please," he said. "Just… come with me."

Tyler didn't speak.

He stood there, eyeing the door.

He glanced at Dillon— the rain picking up, before finally walking over to the car.

He got in.

CHAPTER SEVENTEEN — *What Lies Beneath*

Sunlight returned to Castleton, spilling through the windows of Prescott Estate like it owned the place.

Keegan lay shirtless beneath black silk sheets. His bed—a king-sized monument to indulgence—sat beneath a ceiling mural he'd never actually looked at.

To the world, he looked golden, untouched. To Keegan, it felt like free-falling in slow motion.

He dreamed in snapshots.

Flash

A resort hot tub, steam, diamond watch. A bikini-clad girl slid in beside him like she was born to be there. Of course she was.

Then another **flash**—

Money raining down a staircase. Two girls kissed beneath fluttering bills at one of his extravagant house parties. Chaos. Laughter. Until—

The front door opened. His parents. Home early from a trip to Germany.

His mother: "We leave you here one weekend and you break our trust like this?"

His father: "You're a disappointment, Keegan."

Not the last time he'd hear that.

He remembered prep school—navy blazer, janitor's closet, a girl slipping her bra back on just as the dean barged in.

"What on God's green earth is going on here!?"

Keegan shrugged. Smiled.
"Sorry."

Then came Castleton High. He wore designer sunglasses as he entered his first day, a sea of faded lockers and public school denim.

His parents watched from the car, arms crossed.

Maybe this could be good for him, they'd said.
Build character.

But soon—

The principal's office.

"We're concerned he won't graduate," the counselor said.

At home, just months earlier, Keegan snapped.

"I'm not repeating senior year. I'd rather die than be Castleton's laughingstock."

His mother didn't answer. She just poured herself a shot at the counter.

After that—silence.

The kind that stuck.

His parents were always gone now. World tours. Instagram smiles. Pretending they hadn't raised a mess.

It still hurt.

His brother—off at Yale—barely called anymore.

And then… Heather.

She'd seen past the mask. Not the brand, not the charm—him.

That night at Raven Lake:

"Why do you always do that?" she asked.

"Do what?"

"Act like you're always on. Like the party never stops."

Now, in his dream, Heather returned.

Heather in a white sequined mini dress, kissing him slow. "I see you," she whispered.

Then—

Another mouth traced up his torso before finding his lips. Her dress was… red.

Heather had vanished.

Jane took her place. Hair wild, smile wicked.

"Heather?" he gasped.

Jane pressed a finger to his lips. "Shhh."

He didn't want this. He wanted Heather.

"Heather—please—"

But Jane pushed him backward. He felt himself free-falling again when—

He jolted awake, drenched in sweat. Chest heaving. Sheets twisted.

The sun hadn't moved.

But something inside him had.

Across town, another morning unfolded—less grand, more grounded.

Dillon's room smelled faintly of detergent and cologne. Trophies lined the shelves. A muted cartoon looped on the flatscreen.

On the floor, a trifold mattress was laid out with care. Tyler slept curled up, hoodie bunched under his head.

Dillon leaned over the edge of his bed, rubbing the back of his neck.

Tyler stirred. Blinking. Puffy-eyed.

"Get any rest?" Dillon asked.

"Not really." His voice was hoarse. "Still in shock. Can't believe they actually kicked me out."

He exhaled. "But… what did I expect, right?"

Dillon sat forward.

"For what it's worth," he said gently, "it was brave. Standing up for yourself—for Sam. That took guts."

Tyler let out a hollow laugh. "Yeah. All it got me was a duffel bag and a sidewalk."

Dillon shook his head. "It's 2025. People need to grow up and let go of their homophobic bullshit."

A pause.

Tyler stared at the TV. "Can I ask you something?"

Dillon nodded, bracing.

"Why'd you record me and Sam?"

The question hung heavy.

Dillon sighed. "I was being dumb. When I saw you two… it messed with my head."

He hesitated. "You don't… come across gay, you know? Not the way people expect."

Tyler didn't speak. But the words landed hard.

Dillon rushed to fix it. "That's not an excuse. I panicked. I should've walked away. But I didn't. I hit record like an idiot. That's on me."

Tyler looked away. Then nodded. It wasn't okay. But it was honest.

Dillon stood. "I'll talk to my dad. See if you can stay a while. At least until something more solid comes along."

"You'd do that?"

"Yeah. You're not sleeping on the street."

They exchanged a quiet fist bump.

A start.

Dillon stepped into the hallway, leaving Tyler in the calm of morning light.

Later, at Castleton Coffee House, steam rose from ceramic mugs, and indie music curled around the corners of the café.

Heather and Paige sat by the window with a view of the docks. Sunlight streaked the table.

Paige stirred her drink, quiet. Then—

"He hates me," she said. "Dillon. I just know it."

Heather didn't say anything. She just let the words land.

"I hate who I've become," Paige added, softer. "I don't even recognize myself anymore."

"Stop beating yourself up," said Heather, reaching across the table to take her hand.

Her skin was soft, Heather thought. Sad hands.

"There's something I need to tell you," she said gently.

But the bell above the door jingled.

A breath.

Keegan.

Perfect as always. Crisp tee, effortless charm. He spotted them right away.

He moved over, kissed Heather's cheek.

"Ladies."

Paige caught the flicker in Heather's face. "What were you gonna say?"

Heather hesitated. Then smiled. "It can wait."

Paige gathered her purse and stood. "My mom's probably about to report me missing. I've been crying at Briarwood for days." She laughed softly. "Thanks for being a real friend."

Heather held her hand once more. "Text me when you get home, okay?"

Paige nodded and slipped out.

Keegan slid into the empty seat, his knee bumping Heather's. "I was thinking," he said, "you and me—get away for a few days. Somewhere quiet. Clear our heads."

Heather arched a brow. "It's Labor Day weekend coming up. Everything's gonna be booked."

"Not if you've got an Amex Black Card."

Heather studied him for a long moment. Then—

"I need to tell you something."

His grin faded.

"I'm broke," she said. "Briarwood's going on the market. We're losing everything. I've been faking it for weeks. When you saw me outside this place—the day you told me to invite everyone to your party—I was looking for work."

She braced.

But Keegan smiled.

She blinked. "Why are you smiling?"

"Because you're finally dropping the mask. Like we talked about that day at the lake."

He took her hand. Brushed his thumb over the back of hers. "I don't care about the money. I like you for you."

He leaned in and kissed her—slow, certain, warm.

She closed her eyes. Let it land.

Then, quieter—

"So… you ready to drop yours?"

Keegan looked away out the window. He should've known this would follow. Then he turned back to her.

"My parents?" He exhaled. "They travel to forget I exist. I'm a screw-up. And I think they've stopped trying to fix what's broken."

Heather's expression softened.

He added, "You're the first person who's seen me in a long time."

She tightened her hold. "No matter where this relationship goes," she said, "I've got you. I won't forget you exist. How could I?"

He smiled, almost shy.

"So that's it?" she asked playfully. "That's all that's hiding behind the Keegan Prescott mask?"

Keegan hesitated.

His mind flashed:

The shed.

The red dress.

Jane's breath on his neck.

Back to now.

"I think," he said carefully, "you know all my demons."

But inside, one thought echoed like a siren: *Please, Jane. Keep your mouth shut.*

CHAPTER EIGHTEEN — *Fractures*

The last light of day spilled into EJ's bedroom, stretching across the walls in a faded amber wash. The television glowed in the corner, casting slow-moving shadows across the bed. The volume was low—just background noise. Voices murmuring, light flickering, nothing important.

Molly lay beside EJ, her legs curled on top of his, her eyes on the screen but her thoughts elsewhere. She shifted slightly, laying her head against his shoulder—careful not to wake him.

EJ was asleep.

His breathing was shallow. Uneven.

She glanced down at him. Even in rest, his face looked strained, as if locked in battle with something unseen.

EJ dreamed. A memory—only it didn't feel like memory. It felt like drowning.

Tile floors. Fluorescent lights. Screams that didn't sound real.

Suddenly, he was slammed to the ground. His Harmony High shirt torn and bloodied. His arms pinned by bodies—students, maybe staff. It was hard to tell in the panic. He thrashed wildly, fighting to break free.

"LET ME GO!" he screamed, voice hoarse, lungs burning.

The classroom seemed to be shrinking.

And from the hallway—more shouting.

Then—

A scream.

Jane.

He froze, everything in him clenching.

"NO!" he shouted. "Jane! JANE!"

They held him down like an animal.

He kept screaming as the corridor echoed with chaos. But no one moved.

No one helped.

Everything tilted.

Then—darkness.

Now.

EJ jolted upright, breath sharp and ragged, like he'd surfaced from deep water. Molly flinched slightly, her eyes flying to his face.

"EJ?"

He didn't answer right away. Just stared into the space ahead of him. The blue light from the TV flickered across his skin. His hands trembled in the folds of the blanket.

"EJ," she said again, softer this time. "Are you okay?"

He turned to her slowly, like he wasn't entirely sure where he was.

"I'm— I'm not sure."

They sat in silence for a moment. The television murmured in the background.

Molly stayed quiet. Just there beside him.

For now, that was enough.

In the backyard of the Winthrop house, the evening air had cooled into something quiet and still. EJ and Molly sat on the wooden swing beneath the trees, its slow creaking barely audible over the hum of insects. Stars blinked overhead—silent, distant.

The swing rocked gently, their shoulders brushing now and then. EJ leaned forward, elbows resting on his knees, gaze fixed on the dark lawn.

"I've been dealing with some stuff," he said finally, voice low. "From the town we lived in before. Harmony."

Molly turned slightly, listening without interruption.

"I try to forget it, but sometimes… I can't. The memories just come back." He paused. "Jane got the worst of it. Whatever it did to me—it wrecked her."

Molly studied his profile as he exhaled—slow, shaky.

"When it gets bad, I run. Like, long runs. Just to outrun my own thoughts. I used to do therapy too. For a while." He laughed quietly. "I don't know why I stopped. Sorry—I'm just unloading."

"It's okay," Molly said gently. "You don't have to apologize for feeling things. Sometimes it helps to let it out."

He nodded. "Maybe. But I feel like I have to stay strong. Especially for Jane. I wasn't there for her that day… and I'll never forgive myself for that. I won't let something like that happen again."

"That's why you're so protective of her," Molly said softly.

He looked over at her. "Exactly."

Another pause. His expression darkened.

"But something's off with her now. She's different. Not just mood swings or shutting people out—it's like… she's not even all there sometimes. Like she's fighting something no one else can see."

"What happened in Harmony?" Molly asked quietly.

EJ looked away.

The swing moved slowly beneath them.

"I'm not sure I'm ready to talk about it," he said after a moment.

Molly didn't push. She just reached for his hand, lacing her fingers through his.

"When you are," she said, "I'll be here."

At the Burger Hut, the crowd had thinned to almost nothing. Just minutes from closing, a teenage worker pushed a mop across the greasy tile floor, earbuds in and half-listening to the world.

At a booth near the back, Dillon and Tyler sat across from each other. Wrappers and milkshake cups littered the table. Mr. Powell, still in work boots and a paint-splattered hoodie, sat beside Dillon, nursing a half-empty coffee.

"What are you fellas getting into tomorrow?" he asked, stretching his arms across the bench back.

Dillon glanced at Tyler. "Well, the gym's finally reopening. First time since it flooded. Thought we'd go pump some iron."

"Guess that's the only downside of building a gym that opens up into a Lakefront view," Mr. Powell said, smirking. "Soon as that storm hit, half the weight room turned into a swimming pool."

Tyler stayed mostly quiet during dinner, but he admired the way they talked—the ease between them. A real father-son rhythm. Something he wasn't sure he'd ever have again.

"Thank you again for dinner, Mr. Powell," Tyler said, sitting up a little straighter. "And for letting me stay at your place. It means a lot."

Mr. Powell waved him off with a kind smile. "You're welcome here as long as you need to be, son. We'll figure things out."

Tyler's throat tightened. He didn't feel like he deserved that kind of kindness—but God, he was grateful for it.

He slipped his phone from his pocket, thumb hovering over the screen. For a moment, he hesitated.

Then, quietly, he began typing.

To: Sam

Hey...

CHAPTER NINETEEN — *Burnout*

The morning crowd at Jerry's Fitness Club was already sweating. House beats pounded through the speakers—Josh Baker and Omar+'s "Back It Up" thumping hard enough to shake the free weights. The scent of body spray, pre-workout, and determination clung to the air. Grunts echoed off mirrored walls. The regulars had returned to claim their favorite spots with the grand re-opening.

Then Jane entered.

She didn't just walk in—she arrived.

Her red Bombshell Sportswear gripped her tight. Her low-coverage sports bra left little to the imagination. Her scrunch butt shorts did as intended. She tossed her curls to the side as she scanned her key card at the entrance, the gate clicking open, oversized sunglasses still in place despite the fluorescent lights overhead. She moved through the weight room like a sponsored athlete on a runway as the song seemed to reach a thunderous high.

Jane didn't show up today. She's crying somewhere in a locked drawer. I walked in. DJ, she thought.

A couple guys paused mid-rep. One nearly dropped his barbell. Even the front desk attendant gave a low whistle.

Jane smirked. Let them look.

She wasn't here for them—well, not just them. Today was about release. Releasing pressure. Releasing the ache in her chest. Releasing her.

In the back corner, Keegan spotted her first, mid-rep at the shoulder press.

"You've got to be kidding me. Of course she's here," he muttered under his breath.

Heather, beside him on the rowing machine, turned. Her eyes narrowed. "Jesus, what's in the water at the Winthrop house? They keep getting hotter."

Jane made her way to the squat rack, grabbing a bar and loading on more weight than most would dare for a warm-up. She didn't hesitate. No warm-up set. Just the bar, the breath, the power.

She squatted.

Slow. Controlled.

Heather watched. "She's putting on a show… and I can't stop watching."

Keegan watched too. Apprehension, maybe. Or… familiarity.

"Her chaos phase continues," he said quietly.

Jane may have been steaming up the weight room, but down the tiled corridor in the men's locker room, the actual steam room was doing the same.

Mist curled through the air like breath. The small, dim space was packed—guys lounging on wooden benches, towels slung low at the waist, their bodies slick with sweat and steam. The thump of music from the main room pulsed faintly through the walls, muffled by the hiss of condensation.

Dillon sat back against the wall, muscles relaxed but glistening, his eyes closed, fully at ease. Beside him, Tyler wiped a trail of sweat from his brow and shifted slightly, sneaking a glance at Dillon's abs. It was a mix of curiosity and admiration. His own six-pack wasn't quite where he wanted it to be, not yet.

The heat was thick. Suffocating. Guys shuffled in and out, tapping out from the temperature.

Then the door creaked open again.

Zack.

Pretty-boy Zack. Beach-blond hair, faux humility. Another one of the football guys.

He smirked the moment he saw Tyler.

"Well, would you look at that," Zack said, stepping in. "If my eyes serve me right, Tyler James is blessing us with his presence. Better keep those towels tight, boys—one dick slip and he might get ideas."

Laughter.

Someone chuckled nervously.

Dillon's jaw clenched. He'd heard Zack make jokes before, but this one felt heavier—meaner.

Then suddenly, next to him Tyler launched.

Zack barely had time to blink before Tyler tackled him to the floor, forearm across his throat, fury crackling off him in waves.

"You wanna say that again?" Tyler snarled.

Steam hissed louder, like it was screaming too.

Dillon was on his feet instantly. "Ty—Tyler—stop!"

He yanked him back with force, dragging him off Zack, whose face was red, coughing now.

Zack scrambled to his feet. "You're fucking crazy!"

Dillon didn't even look at him. "Shut up, Zack."

He shoved open the steam room door and pulled Tyler out into the cooler air of the locker room.

Tyler paced like a caged animal.

Dillon stared him down. "You can't keep doing that."

Tyler didn't respond at first. His chest was still heaving, his fists trembling at his sides. But underneath the anger, something else flared—humiliation.

"He deserved it," Tyler snapped.

"Maybe. But you can't go flying off the handle every time someone says or does some dumb shit. People are gonna talk."

"Let them," Tyler said. "Fuck him."

In the distance, Keegan shut his locker harder than necessary. If Jane said even a word to Heather about that night in the shed… he wasn't just screwed. He was exposed.

From the boys' room into the girls', the locker room had quieted.

Jane stood near the mirror, fluffing her curls, the sharp click of her compact echoing lightly. She dabbed a final swipe of lipstick—blush red, glossy, perfect.

Heather walked up, towel slung over her shoulder.

"Looking good, Winthrop. You never used to stand out… but you're giving everything now."

Jane cracked a smile in the mirror. "Really?"

"Really," Heather said. "Nice lipstick, by the way."

Jane, dramatic as ever, spun around. "Oh my God, thank you! I just picked it up from Ulta. Want to try it?"

Heather tossed her hair. "Obviously."

Jane stood and gestured toward the bench. "Sit."

Heather did.

Jane straddled her—facing her—legs on both sides, close but careful, the room now nearly empty.

Heather didn't stop her—but her breath caught, just slightly.

It was Jane's game now.

Jane leaned forward, carefully tracing the lipstick onto Heather's lips.

Then, Jane tilted to the side so Heather could see herself in the large mirror behind her.

"You like it?"

Heather held her gaze. "More than you realize."

Jane's lips curled. Then, slowly—deliberately—she leaned in.

Heather didn't stop her.

They kissed. Slow. Measured. Intimate.

Heather knew this was dangerous, but the way Jane looked at her… it was easier not to care.

Jane pulled back, lips glinting. "How was that?"

Heather exhaled. "Familiar."

Jane stood. "Familiar for who? You… or Keegan? Considering he's tasted these lips."

Heather's expression broke.

"What did you just say?"

Jane spun on her heel. "You heard me. Keegan's tasted these lips— and then some."

Jane paused at the doorway, tossing her hair. "He's had a taste of cake, too—hell, the whole damn bakery."

She smirked. "Toodles."

Heather sat stiff on the bench, lipstick still fresh, trying to sort the heat from the hurt.

And failing.

Her face red with simmering anger and fists tight… she knew, because the mirror she stared at didn't lie.

CHAPTER TWENTY— *Let Them Look*

The sun dipped low over Raven Lake, painting Castleton in gold streaks. Inside Sam's house, he stood before a full-length mirror, straightening the collar of his button-up for the third time. His reflection looked calm, but his heart was not.

Behind him, Maria leaned against the doorframe, arms crossed. She didn't speak at first—just watched with the kind of silence that came from growing up together.

"You sure you're up for this?" she asked, stepping forward. Her voice was soft but carried weight. "Not too soon for a date with him?"

Sam glanced at her in the mirror. "I wouldn't call it a date," he said. "We just... miss each other. This feels like a way to see where we stand."

Maria moved closer and wrapped her arms around him. Their eyes met in the reflection.

"I love you, you know."

Sam swallowed. He covered her hands with his own.
"I love you too."

"It's been a rough road," she said, resting her chin on his shoulder. "The outing. The comments. The silence."

Sam nodded. "It's been... a lot. But I can't ignore how I feel about him. Or how he feels about me. I don't know where it's going. We'll see."

Maria squeezed him. "Whatever happens, I'm here."

Their reflections stood still in the fading light—caught between past and maybe.

Outside, headlights swept across the drive. A car pulled up, engine low.

Maria stepped back. "Go. Stay safe. And follow your heart."

Sam exhaled and grabbed his jacket. "Always."

He opened the front door just as Tyler looked up from behind the wheel of Dillon's car. Their eyes met through the windshield. Hope. Or history.

Across town, the stars crept out one by one. Heather sat alone at the edge of the dock, her feet just above the dark lake water. The boards beneath her creaked with the weight of memory.

She didn't move when Keegan appeared.

She didn't need to.

"Is it true?" she asked.

Keegan stayed behind her. "What?"

Her voice tightened. "Don't play dumb. Did you sleep with her?"

Silence.

"Jane," she said. "Damn it."

Keegan's breath hitched. He knew this was coming.

"Yes," he said.

The word split the air—not because she didn't already know, but because knowing and hearing are different kinds of pain.

"How was it?" she asked. Eyes forward. Voice flat.

Keegan winced. "Heather, don't."

She turned, moonlight washing over her face.

"I thought we were real."

"We are," he said. "It was a wild night. Bad decisions. She pulled me in and—" He stopped. Shook his head. "It just happened."

Heather's jaw set. "Not that simple."

She stood, facing him now. Her voice wavered, but her spine didn't.

"I bared all for you. You're the only guy I ever trusted enough to see me. All of me."

"I know," he said. "And you saw me too. More than I deserved."

She looked away, then back again. "Is that enough?"

Keegan stepped forward. Slow. Careful.

"It can be."

But when he reached for her, she stepped back.

"I need space."

She walked past him, cold.

Keegan stood at the edge, alone with the dark water.

Downtown Burlington, Vermont buzzed. Warm city lights glowed in the night. Music spilled from open doorways. Sam and Tyler walked side by side—roughly an hour outside Castleton, but it felt like another world.

Tyler had planned the trip. He remembered Sam always said he loved it here.

He was right.

"I still want to go to school here," Sam said as they passed a row of shops. "UVM. It still feels right."

Tyler nodded. "I like it here too. No judging faces."

They moved through the crowd, shoulders brushing. Then—without thinking—they reached for each other's hands.

Fingers laced.

Tyler's voice dropped. "My insecurities... they put us through hell. I'm sorry."

Sam looked at him. "I forgave you. You don't have to keep saying it."

Tyler's eyes shimmered. "I just want to do better. For you. For me."

Sam reached up and wiped a tear from Tyler's cheek. "You are."

Then—

Tyler kissed Sam.

Right there on the sidewalk.

Nobody stared. Nobody whispered.

Just footsteps. Guitar strings. The night holding them softly.

When they pulled back, Sam smiled.

"Did Tyler James just kiss me in public?" he asked. "A very busy public?"

Tyler kissed him again. Firmer. A vow.

"Let them look."

Sam could've melted.

So he did.

CHAPTER TWENTY-ONE — *Echoes from the Past*

E.J. sat alone in the softly lit waiting room, fingers laced tight in his lap. A wall clock ticked overhead—each second slow, deliberate. The Castleton Wellness Center smelled faintly of lemon cleaner and burnt coffee.

The door opened with a quiet click.

Dr. Alston stepped out, clipboard in hand. "E.J.," he said with a kind smile. "Come on in."

They moved to a modest office—neutral walls, a window overlooking some trees, two chairs angled just enough to suggest safety without pressure. E.J. sat. So did Dr. Alston.

"Dr. Crane sent your file over," the therapist said, setting the clipboard aside. "I understand you'd like to continue your sessions here in Castleton, not back in Harmony?"

E.J. nodded, his throat tight. "Yeah. I've been… having dreams. Not even dreams. Nightmares. About that day."

Dr. Alston let the silence stretch, inviting more.

"You want to tell me about it?"

E.J. looked down, then away, his mind dragging him back—past the office walls, past the trees outside, past Castleton entirely.

A memory…

Flash…

Jane in her cheer uniform, tugging at her sleeve. "I don't know, E… something feels off about today."

"It's probably just nerves," E.J. had said, trying to reassure her. "You've got a competition coming up."

"I'm serious. I don't know how else to describe it."

E.J. had nodded, still skeptical. "Alright. I'll go check on Johnny."

Johnny.

That name still echoed like a siren underwater.

He blinked hard.

Back in the office, Dr. Alston waited, calm and steady.

E.J. stared at his hands. They weren't shaking—but it felt like they should be.

At the local bookstore in Castleton's town square, fingers trailed the spines of books already read. Sam.

Hearts still in his eyes, head still somewhere in Burlington.

Then—

A head popped around the corner.

"Heather?" he said, surprised. "Pretty sure you're in the wrong section," he teased, nodding toward the Pride flag over the section.

She smirked. "Actually, I wanted to talk. Somewhere a little more… discreet."

Sam raised a brow. What could Heather Briarwood possibly want with him?

They settled near the window, iced drinks sweating on the table. Heather stirred her iced caramel macchiato, eyes flicking to the street outside.

"You're the only person I know who's out," she said. "Or at least the only one I feel comfortable talking to."

Sam leaned in, mock-serious. "Go on. I'm listening."

Heather hesitated.

"How did you know you were gay?"

He blinked. "It's just always been what it is. It's not like I decided to go down this road with so many obstacles—I just… knew."

She looked down. "I've been wronged recently. By someone I care about deeply. And I know he cares about me too, but honestly, I haven't exactly been the best girlfriend myself."

Sam nodded, fully tuned in.

"But," she continued, "I also have feelings for…"

Sam braced for the name.

"*Her*," Heather said, purposely evading.

Sam's eyes widened. "Oh, honey. Spill it."

Heather smiled but shook her head. "I need to talk to her first."

"Respect," Sam said, holding up his hands.

Heather sighed. "I guess I'm saying I have feelings for both. A boy and a girl. I like them both. And it feels… natural. But maybe I'm confused."

Sam softened. "Sounds to me like Heather Briarwood might be bisexual. But hey, that's your label to claim—or not. Either way, it's fun under the rainbow. We'd love to have you."

Heather laughed. "You're much too much."

Sam's phone buzzed. A text from Maria. As he replied, Heather pulled out her own phone, smiling at a photo in her album of her with… Paige.

Afternoon light sliced across Dillon's bedroom in warm streaks. Tyler lay tangled on the trifold mattress, sheets twisted, dreams forgotten.

Dillon leaned over the side of his bed. "Rise and shine, sleepyhead."

Tyler groaned, rubbing his eyes. Still drained from the Burlington trip. From everything.

"So?" Dillon asked. "How'd last night go?"

Tyler rolled onto his back. "Better than expected," he said softly. "It was kind of… special."

He hesitated, then added, "Hey—I meant what I said. I'm gonna fill your gas tank when I start at Burger Hut. Help with the bills."

Dillon gave him a look—half amused, half sincere. "You don't have to do that."

"I want to," Tyler said, sitting up. "It means something."

But before Dillon could answer, the door burst open.

Bootsteps. Voices.

Two officers entered the room. Mr. Powell followed, face lined with worry.

"Wait—what's going on?" Dillon said, jumping up.

One officer, a woman, stepped forward. "Are you Tyler James?"

Tyler rose slowly. "I am."

She met his gaze. "You're under arrest for aggravated assault."

Tyler's breath caught. "I didn't do anything."

"The video says otherwise," she replied, already reaching for the cuffs. "Turn around."

Dillon stepped forward. "This is bullshit. He didn't—"

"Dillon," Mr. Powell cut in, holding out an arm. "Let them do what they have to do. We'll fix this."

Mr. Powell turned to Tyler. "We'll get a lawyer. Don't say anything until then."

The cuffs clicked shut.

Tyler didn't fight it. He just stood there—like his body was happening without him—as they read him his rights.

His mind buzzed.

Where does it all go from here?

But all he could hear was the sound of that glass table breaking. Over and over again.

CHAPTER TWENTY-TWO — *Charged*

In the void—black, endless, and silent—Jane stood. Her hair was pulled back into a perfect ponytail, not a strand out of place. Blouse, cardigan, soft blush—classic Jane. But the calm was a costume. Behind her wide eyes, there was fear.

"Let me out!" she screamed into the dark. "If you hear me, I'm getting stronger. I'm coming back to reclaim what's mine!"

A cackle echoed from the shadows.

Her reflection emerged—not the prim one, but the other. The one with the wild curls. Red jumper. Devilish grin between the cherry gloss.

"Your threats are empty, honey," the alter said, dragging a sliding cell door into view. "DJ is here to stay. This is my show now."

CLANG.

The gate slammed shut—

—and we're no longer in her mind.

A real gate slams. Tyler flinches.

He's in a cell. Breathing heavy. The world returns suddenly and sharply.

He sat on the narrow bench, the chill of the metal seeping through his jeans. Across the bars, a policewoman jotted notes on a clipboard.

"Why am I even here?" Tyler asked, his voice low, cracked.

She didn't look up right away.

"We told you, Mr. James. Aggravated assault."

Her tone was practiced. Emotionless.

"The video got around—it's clear what happened. Someone reported it. You shoved him into a glass table. He blacked out. Probable cause caught on camera."

Tyler blinked. "But… Sam didn't press charges."

"You're not being charged by Sam," she replied. "You're being charged by the state. That's how it works when it crosses into felony assault."

She turned and walked away, boots clicking against the tile.

Tyler stared after her, hollow.

A single tear slipped down his cheek. He didn't wipe it.

It's over, he thought.

I finally had something good… and now it's gone.

In the police station lobby, Dillon paced near the vending machines. He hadn't sat once.

"Is he getting out?" he asked again.

Mr. Powell didn't glance up from his phone. "I'm working on it."

"That's what you said an hour ago."

"I've got the lawyer on the line. Just give me a minute."

But Dillon didn't want to wait. He didn't want to sit still. He wanted to rip the cuffs off Tyler with his bare hands. He shoved through the lobby door and stepped outside.

The air hit sharp. Cool and unwelcome.

"Dillon."

He turned.

Paige stood at the curb, hesitant.

"What are you doing here?" he snapped.

"I came to see if he's okay. I saw him in the backseat, driving through town."

"Oh, now you care?" His voice cracked. "You're the reason this happened."

Her brows pulled together, shocked. "Excuse me? If we're pointing fingers, let's not forget *you're* the one who recorded that night. That video started this."

He looked away, jaw tight. "I didn't mean for it to get out."

"But it did," Paige said. "And now he's the one in a cell while we all stand here blaming each other."

They fell silent. Breathing hard.

"We can't live in the past," she said finally. "We need to get him out. Does Sam even know?"

Dillon shook his head. "It happened so fast. I don't think so."

Paige pulled out her phone. "Then we need to tell him. Now."

She tapped his name. Put it on speaker.

As the line rang, Dillon looked across the street.

A boy in jeans and a plaid button-up stood watching them.

Paige followed his gaze. "Dillon?"

Dillon's stomach dropped.

Zack.

His teammate. The one who joked in the steam room. The one Tyler attacked. The one who was watching them now, lips pressed in something too smug to be innocent.

And then—Zack turned and walked away.

Dillon knew. Fury flashed across his face.

He'd found the snitch.

CHAPTER TWENTY-THREE — *Release*

Dear Diary,

Castleton isn't at all what I expected. It's picture-perfect on the outside, like a postcard I'd send back to relatives in Mill Valley—but underneath? There's pain. Hurt. Secrets.

I didn't think I'd get caught in any of it, but here I am—trying to stay strong for a boyfriend who's clearly haunted. Haunted by something that happened before he moved here himself.

And his sister... Jane. Sweet, innocent Jane. Only now it's like she's changed. There's a darkness in her eyes I never noticed before. Like she's someone else entirely.

And then there's Heather. God, Heather. She came after me like it was sport—like tearing someone down makes her feel taller. She tried to break me. But I didn't break. Because E.J. and I... we love each other. We do. And that love held.

But still, something's missing.

I don't feel completely with him yet. Not with this secret hanging between us. I can feel it. Like fog he can't see through. I just hope one day he trusts me enough to let it out—to let me in.

He started therapy again. Maybe that's the first step.

Maybe.

Molly closed the diary and placed it gently on her nightstand. Now in pajamas, she moved to the window, gazing next door through the dark. From here, she had a perfect view of E.J.'s room.

He was there. Lit by the soft glow of his desk lamp.

She watched as he pulled off his shirt—revealing his body, not his soul. He tossed it into the laundry basket with a hollow thud, his shoulders heavy, like he was carrying something no one else could see.

How on earth is he supposed to be up for the camping trip? she wondered.

What he really needed wasn't a night under the stars.

It was a release.

E.J. sat on the edge of his bed, elbows on his knees, staring at the floor like it held answers.

The silence was thick—broken only by the soft mechanical hum of his desk fan oscillating side to side. He'd tossed his shirt in the basket without thinking, but now he was cold. Not from the air, but from inside. Like something had drained from his blood and never returned.

The echo still rang in his mind.

Jane's scream. Johnny's name.

His chest tightened. Anger surged up his throat like bile.

He snapped.

"Why did this have to happen to us!"

He shot up, grabbed the desk fan, and hurled it across the room.

CRASH.

Metal hit drywall. Plastic shattered. The hum fell silent.

Within seconds, footsteps thundered up the stairs.

His door burst open—Mr. and Mrs. Winthrop rushed in, eyes wide.

E.J. collapsed. Knees hit carpet.

And then he was crying—**not silently, not holding back—but raw, broken, in his mother's arms.**

Across town at the Castleton Jail, another boy sat just as wrecked—but masked it the best way he knew how.

"I'm not pressing charges," Sam said firmly.

He sat across from a uniformed officer in a small interview room, posture tight but composed.

The officer nodded slowly, leaning back in his chair. "I hear you. But your decision doesn't determine whether charges move forward. In cases like this, especially with evidence like that video, the state steps in. The DA makes the call. You're the victim—but the case belongs to the people of this state."

Sam frowned. "So it doesn't matter what I want?"

"It matters," the officer said. "Just not in the way you think."

Sam leaned forward, voice low. "I won't testify against him."

A beat passed between them.

"At least Tyler's getting out tonight, right?"

The officer turned and glanced through the glass window. In the lobby, Mr. Powell stood talking to another officer.

"That's likely already in motion," he said.

Relief spread across Sam's face—quiet, but visible.

At the front desk, the officer asked, "Are you Tyler James's legal guardian?"

Mr. Powell hesitated, then replied with calm conviction. "Not officially, no. But I've been the one feeding him, housing him. His parents haven't been in the picture for a while."

The officer nodded, jotting it down. "That's all I needed. You'll be listed on the release paperwork."

In the lobby, Dillon and Paige leaned side by side against a wall, their phones forgotten for once. The silence between them wasn't cold —it was cautious and guarded.

"I think he's getting out," Paige said, nodding toward the hallway.

Dillon followed her gaze. "About time."

They both looked toward Mr. Powell who seemed to have a half smile on his face, a sharp contrast to the rest of the day. They leaned forward slightly, instinctively aligned. It wasn't a full repair—but maybe a crack in the wall was enough for now.

The door opened, and they braced for Tyler.

It was Sam.

He walked toward them, his usual bravado replaced with something gentler.

"Thanks," Sam said, glancing at Dillon. "For letting him crash with you."

Dillon shrugged. "Wasn't a problem. I've got his back."

And then the doors opened again.

This time, it was Tyler.

Hair messy. Eyes clear.

As soon as they saw him, the group moved in.

Hugs and quiet relief.

For the first time in a long time, it didn't feel like everything was falling apart.

It felt like—maybe—it was starting to fall back together.

For now.

.

CHAPTER TWENTY-FOUR — *Please, Don't Leave Me*

The late night was cooler than usual, a quiet signal that fall was approaching fast.

Dillon walked beside Paige along the empty sidewalk, their pace unhurried. Streetlamps glowed in long intervals, and the houses they passed were mostly dark. It was one of those walks where neither of them had planned what to say—and for once, that felt okay.

"I'm partly to blame," Paige finally said, breaking the silence. "For everything."

Dillon nodded. "Same."

She looked over at him, her eyes soft but guarded. "We can be better."

He smiled faintly. "I want to."

They reached her porch, and both paused. Porch light flickering. The world quiet.

For a heartbeat, Dillon leaned in just slightly. So did she. A subtle shift. Breath caught between them.

But neither moved further.

Instead, Paige gave a sheepish smile and opened the door.

"Hope my mom doesn't kill me for being out this late," she said.

"Tell her I was your bodyguard."

"Sure. That'll go over well." She laughed lightly. Then, as she stepped inside, she looked back. "Get home safe, D."

He let a smile cross his face, watching her beauty.

She shut the door gently behind her.

In her room, Paige tossed her jacket onto a chair and sank onto her bed. Her phone buzzed.

Heather: Can I come over? Can't sleep.

Paige replied without hesitation. Of course.

Outside the Powell home, Tyler stood with his hands in his pockets, eyes on the stars.

Sam stepped closer beside him. The silence between them had shifted—not empty, just full of things unspoken.

"I told the officer," Sam said, voice low. "I'm not pressing charges. And I'm not testifying either."

Tyler looked over, eyes tired. "It's not up to you, though."

Sam gave a sad smile. "Maybe not. But it still matters."

They stood side by side in the cool night air.

"I wish we could just disappear," Sam said.

Tyler nodded. "Yeah. Me too."

They turned toward each other, and without another word, they leaned in and kissed—soft, long, and slow. The kind of kiss that didn't erase anything, but quieted it for a moment.

Footsteps crunched up the gravel path.

"Okay, get a room, you two," Dillon called, smirking as he reached the front steps.

Tyler and Sam broke apart laughing, their foreheads still touching.

"Goodnight, Dillon," Tyler said, mock-serious.

Dillon gave a mock salute and headed inside.

Tyler kissed Sam again—this time brief, grateful.

At Paige's window, a gentle knock sounded.

She got out of bed and walked over, cracked it open, and found Heather in leggings and an oversized hoodie.

"My mom's knocked out hard," Paige whispered. "Thank God… I just got home."

Heather climbed in quietly and sat on the edge of the bed, legs pulled up underneath her.

"Tyler's out," Paige offered gently, watching for a reaction.

Heather gave a small nod but didn't speak right away. Paige sat beside her, close but not touching.

"What's wrong?" Paige asked. "You look like you haven't slept in days."

"Everything," Heather breathed. "It's all wrong."

She stared ahead at nothing in particular.

"The house is still there," she said after a moment. "We saved Briarwood. Daddy managed to pull some strings. Settled the debt. Paid off the lien. All that estate drama… gone. We get to keep the house."

"That's good though, right?" Paige asked gently.

Heather shook her head. "It should be. But now it just feels like… a shell. Like the structure is still standing, but everything inside— what it meant—is gone. Almost everything was sold."

She reached out slowly, almost like she didn't notice she was doing it, and curled her fingers around Paige's hand.

"I feel like everything's being taken away from me," she said. "All my things at Briarwood. Keegan. And I know I'm hard to be around. I know I push people."

Heather paused.

"Paige... the only thing I have left is you."

The words lingered in the air.

Paige didn't move. She felt the weight of them. The honesty. The ache.

"You know I'm here for you," Paige said softly. "I've been here for you since I moved to this town."

"Don't leave me," Heather whispered.

Paige's heart fluttered—not romantically, just... protectively.

"I won't," she said. "Trust me."

Heather's eyes locked onto hers, wide and glassy. Then she leaned in and kissed her.

Paige froze. Just for a second.

Heather pulled back immediately. "I'm sorry."

Paige blinked, searching for something to say. "It's okay. I... I know you're going through a lot."

There was quiet between them.

Then Heather leaned in again, slower this time.

Paige didn't pull away.

They kissed—tentative, breath-held. Like two people figuring out in real time what it meant to need someone.

CHAPTER TWENTY-FIVE — *The Morning-After*

Late morning slid in slow, filtering through the slats of Paige's blinds like liquid gold. The room was quiet except for the hum of the ceiling fan and the gentle rustle of sheets. Heather lay beside Paige, one arm curled above her head, hair cascading across the pillow like spilled ink.

Paige was already awake. Barely moving. Just breathing in the silence. Letting the weight of the night settle behind her eyes. Too much happened in the last 24 hours she thought.

Paige then sat up and moved across the room, barefoot and careful.

Pulled the blinds back.

"She's gone," she murmured, scanning the driveway. "Mom left for work already."

She let the blinds snap shut and flopped back onto the mattress. The bedsprings groaned softly beneath her.

Heather stirred behind her. "Thanks for letting me crash."

"Anytime," Paige replied, still staring at the ceiling.

A pause. The kind that meant something else was coming.

Heather rolled onto her back. Stared up.

"So... are we gonna talk about that kiss?" she asked, tone casual— but too casual to be innocent.

Paige smirked faintly. "We don't have to."

She turned on her side, her voice light, her face unreadable. "It was a moment of grief and needing. I get it."

She looked over. "Right?"

Heather sat up slowly, pulling her knees to her chest. The sunlight carved gold onto the edge of her collarbone.

"Maybe a little of that," she said. "But I should be honest."

She turned toward Paige.

"I have feelings for you."

Paige blinked. Just once. She didn't panic. But her whole body felt like it was listening.

"Like the ones you have for Keegan?" she asked quietly.

Heather scoffed, half a laugh. "Keegan cheated on me with Jane. Of all people."

Then, with a shrug: "Though I'll admit—she's got that whole sultry, ice-princess thing going now. It's kinda hot."

Paige laughed, shaking her head as she stood and wandered into the kitchen.

From the other room: "Don't act like you wouldn't take Keegan back."

Heather crossed to the mirror, sunlight spilling across her as she twisted her hair up into a perfectly undone bun.

"I would," Heather admitted. "But not without conditions. He needs to reflect. Suffer a little. Know what he lost. Know that cheating on me was the dumbest thing he's ever done."

Paige returned with a bitten apple in hand, still chewing. "So what are you going on about, then?"

Heather stepped toward her. Slowly.

"The way I want him," she said. "That pull—I feel it for you too."

Paige stopped chewing.

"You're serious?"

Heather nodded, her gaze soft but direct.

"It's not just sexual. You're more than that. You're home. My best friend. But if I'm being real... there's a part of me that wants more."

There was no tension. Just something charged and suspended in the air between them.

Heather reached out, slowly, and took the apple from Paige's hand. Bit into it.

Crunch.

Juice ran down the edge of her mouth. She didn't wipe it. Her eyes never left Paige's.

"I have feelings for you," she repeated—this time like she knew exactly what it meant.

Paige blinked again. Quiet. Processing.

Then—

Paige asked. "Have you ever kissed a girl before me?"

Heather smiled faintly. "Yeah. Once. One of Keegan's parties. He was at the top of the stairs making it rain—like some hip-hop Jesus—and I kissed this girl under a rain of twenties. She was from out of town. Never saw her again. Never talked about it."

"You think Keegan saw you? Does he know it was you that kissed that girl?"

"If he did, he never said."

Paige smirked. "What if he wanted to see you with another girl?"

Heather turned slowly back to the mirror.

And then—her reflection blurred. The room shifted. Color saturated. Time slowed.

Keegan sat on the edge of a bed—shirtless, his favorite boxer briefs, hair tousled. A smug smirk playing on his lips. Neon light washed everything in violet and gold.

Heather straddled his thigh, dragging her fingers up his chest. She leaned in, kissed him—languid, familiar.

From behind him, Paige's arms wrapped around his shoulders. Her lips found Keegan's neck. Her fingers hooked into his waistband.

Then—Heather met Paige's eyes.

Paused.

And leaned over Keegan, kissing her.

Soft. Long. Like she'd done it a thousand times. Like she never had.

Keegan leaned back slightly—watching, breath caught in his throat.

Heather and Paige tangled in front of him. His fantasy made flesh.

Back in the Room

Heather blinked.

She was back in Paige's bedroom, staring at her reflection.

She bit into the apple again, like nothing happened.

"Oh, he'd get his rocks off."

Paige let out a laugh, brushing hair behind her ear. "So go call him, psycho."

Heather shrugged. "Maybe I will."

But Paige's voice softened.

"Jokes aside—I liked kissing you. It was different. Good, even. But I'm still strictly dickly."

She hesitated.

"I still want Dillon."

Heather nodded. No drama. No performance.

"I figured."

"You okay with that?"

"Of course." A beat. Then: "Doesn't change how I feel about you. Doesn't change that I love you."

Paige smiled, warm and clear.

"Girl, boy—whoever you're with—I've got you. You're still mine."

Heather looked at her reflection again. This time, it smiled back.

"I'll remember that."

A couple blocks away, at the Powell house, the TV murmured in the background—*American Dad*, played out in bright flickers across the screen.

Tyler lay on the trifold mattress on Dillon's floor, scrolling absently through his phone, his thumbs moving slower than his thoughts. Dillon laid leg-up on his bed, he knew this episode by hard.

There was a knock.

Both boys looked toward the door.

Mr. Powell's voice came through. Calm but serious.

"Tyler? Can you come to the den? You've got a visitor."

Tyler and Dillon locked eyes.

Tyler sat up, tossed his phone aside. He grabbed the T-shirt crumpled beside him and pulled it on over his head. His pulse was already picking up, but he didn't let it show. He left the room without a word.

Dillon watched the door Tyler had walked through. The TV flickered. He stared, eyes clouded.

"Second chance," he muttered. "Better not blow it."

In the den, sunlight filtered through the heavy curtains, making the room feel warmer than it was.

A man in his forties—rumpled tie, tired eyes, holding a worn leather folder—stood waiting beside Mr. Powell.

"Tyler," the man said, offering a hand. "I'm Mark Estrada. I'm with the Public Defender's office."

Tyler shook it, stiffly.

Mr. Estrada flipped open the folder and got right to it.

"Because the victim—Sam—is refusing to testify or cooperate, the State has decided to drop the charges."

Tyler blinked. The words floated for a second before they landed.

"Wait—seriously?" he asked. "It's over?"

Mr. Estrada held up a finger.

"It's not a clean slate," he said. "It's a second chance. With conditions."

Tyler's smile faded.

Mr. Estrada continued, reading from the folder like it wasn't the first time today.

"You've been placed in a pretrial diversion program. That means no conviction goes on your record—as long as you complete all the required steps."

Tyler nodded, slower now.

"Which are?"

"First: mandatory counseling. Anger management and violence prevention. You'll need to attend weekly sessions and check in with your diversion supervisor—here's his card."

He handed over a small laminated card. Tyler took it quietly.

"Second: a written apology to Sam. Honest. Specific. No B.S."

Tyler exhaled.

"Third: twenty hours of community service. Most likely tied to youth programs or violence prevention initiatives. You'll get your assignment by next week."

Tyler nodded again, more robotic now.

"And finally," Estrada added, flipping to the last page, "a temporary no contact order."

Tyler's head snapped up. "Wait—what? Me and Sam are good. Like... really good."

"I don't make the rules, Mr. James," Estrada said. "But I'd advise you to follow them. Because failure to comply means…"

He let the sentence hang.

Mr. Powell finished it: "The original charges get reinstated. And the DA comes for your throat."

Tyler stared at the floor.

He felt a strange blend of relief and something colder— something that sat at the base of his throat like a stone.

He was free.

But it didn't feel like freedom.

He glanced at the card again. The name stared back at him. So did the weight of what came next.

On the opposite side of town at Sam's, the kitchen was a mess of camping gear—coolers, folded tarps, tangled flashlights, and mismatched sleeping bags spread out across the table and countertops. Sam stood at the island sorting through it all with Maria, both of them slightly overwhelmed by the chaos. Music softly playing from the radio.

His mom moved around the kitchen with a soft hum, organizing snacks and taping names onto water bottles.

"Aunt Jessica," Maria said, lifting a folded tent. "Thank you, you really came through with all these supplies."

Jessica smiled. "I took a camping trip like this once. Mine was a bit chaotic but I'm sure you all will enjoy it and have the best time."

A sharp ring from the doorbell pulled her out of the kitchen.

"I've got it," she called, already halfway to the front door.

The radio continued to play faintly, something soft— 'Til Tuesday's "Voices Carry." Appropriate, given the silence in the room.

Sam picked up a flashlight, clicked it on, then off again. The beam flared against the ceiling for a second before fading.

"Honestly?" he said. "I don't even feel like going."

Maria looked at Sam as he continued.

"I mean, last night… looking up at the stars with Tyler? That felt like enough. I don't need to do it again in the middle of the woods."

Maria didn't smile. She placed the tent down carefully.

"I'm glad you and Tyler are in a good place," she said. "Really. But I want you to be careful."

She lowered her voice, just in case her aunt was on her way back.

"The whole incident with you. And I heard he attacked Zack in the gym steam room too."

Sam's face tightened. "Zack provoked him. He was being awful. I'm pretty sure he's the one who tipped the cops off about the video too."

Maria didn't argue. She just looked at him, steady.

"Even so. Tyler's got an aggressive side. That doesn't go away just because someone says sorry."

Sam didn't answer.

Maria stepped closer.

"I like Tyler. I do. But I like you more. That's all this is."

"You didn't like him so much in the hospital that night when you came out swinging."

They both laugh.

"And I'd do it again if I ever feel you're wronged. I'm not saying don't love him. I'm not even saying don't forgive him. But just… move slow. Please. You're my favorite cousin. My best friend. I'm just looking out for you."

Sam looked at her. Really looked.

His throat bobbed, but he didn't speak right away.

Then, quietly: "Yeah. I hear you."

A beat.

"I promise. I'll figure this all out."

CHAPTER TWENTY-SIX — *Unhealed Wounds*

The sun dipped low over Castleton, casting golden light across the still shoreline. The dock creaked softly where it met the lake. E.J. sat at the edge, sneakers dangling inches above the rippling surface. A quiet breeze tugged at his sleeves as he stared out, eyes locked on the horizon like it might offer answers.

Behind him, footsteps approached. Molly eased down beside him, two glass soda bottles in hand. She passed him one without a word.

"Big day tomorrow," she said, trying to keep it casual. "You ready for the camping trip?"

E.J. gave a short laugh—but it didn't reach his eyes.

"Not really," he said. Then: "There's something I've been meaning to tell you. Something I should've told you a long time ago."

Molly turned toward him. "Okay," she said softly. "Whenever you're ready."

He stared at the dock boards, then the lake. Then finally at her.

"I don't want there to be secrets between us."

She reached over and took his hand. Held it.

"It's about Johnny," he said. "The brother I mentioned I had."

Molly nodded. "Your half-brother with Jane."

E.J. swallowed. "Yeah. Same dad, different mom. His mom went to prison. But that's not the story."

She didn't interrupt.

"We used to live in a town called Harmony," E.J. said. "Not far from here, but it might as well be another planet. That place… it broke everything."

Molly sat still, listening.

"Johnny never really fit in. Not with us, not at school. My mom tried. Dad tried. Jane and I too. But Johnny… he always felt like an outsider. Like he didn't want to belong. Maybe it was the fact we were half siblings and he didn't want to connect as much, but over time, that did something to him."

E.J. rubbed his hands together, knuckles tight.

"He had mood swings. Tics. Stuff you'd brush off as quirks until it got darker. There was one time he broke a kid's nose during gym. But that seemed to pale in comparison to everything else that followed."

Molly wondered how it could get worse.

"He shattered the windshield of our neighbor's car with a crowbar because he thought they were spying on him. Said he saw them watching from their blinds. Another time… he killed their cat. Buried it in our backyard because he was feeling stress and claimed he needed to release it somehow."

Molly stiffened slightly. E.J. noticed—but kept going.

"We were scared. We didn't know what to do. But none of that prepared us for what happened next."

His voice dropped.

"I was a sophomore. Johnny was a freshman. Jane was still in eighth grade—bright, bubbly, full of light. She was visiting Harmony High that day for orientation. The middle school kids had come to tour the school."

He blinked, as if trying to dislodge the images forming.

"Johnny said he was sick. Told our parents he was staying home. But he didn't."

Molly's grip on his hand tightened.

"He showed up anyway. In combat boots. Black trench coat. A duffel bag. Walked straight into the library where the visiting middle schoolers were… but he wasn't there for them. He saw the guys who had been severely bully him for years near a row of computers."

E.J. looked at Molly, voice cracking.

"He had a gun."

Molly's lips parted. No words came.

"Jane saw him pull it from the bag but it was too late. He shot all of them. Somehow, in the midst of the chaos that ensued , Riley, one of Jane's classmates was shot. She tried to help him when he stumbled towards her, but he didn't make it. Blood on her uniform. In her hair."

E.J. exhaled, shaking.

"She crawled under a table. Another student, Tate, hid beside her. He asked what was happening, but Jane couldn't speak. He panicked, then suddenly something snapped inside her and she told him to shut up."

Molly's eyes filled, but she said nothing.

"I was outside on the track. PE. We heard the shots and everyone scattered. But I ran toward the building. I knew Jane was inside."

E.J. stared ahead, hollow.

"I saw him in the hallway. Johnny. Rifle raised. He shot another kid, Liam. I later found out that was his name. I tried to help the boy, but I couldn't stop the bleeding, it was too much. I screamed for help. But then I saw Jane."

He paused.

"She had left the library, convinced that maybe she was the one that could talk Johnny down—just maybe."

Molly's breath hitched.

"We were on opposite ends of the hallway. I felt miles apart from Jane. Johnny turned to her and said he didn't think she'd be there today. That he didn't want her to see any of this. I tried get up from the ground and run to her, but someone—staff, other students—I don't even know who—they pulled me in a room. I tried to break free from there grips but then I was slammed down to the ground. I did everything I could to get to my sister… to Jane. I was trapped."

He swallowed hard.

"Then I heard a gunshot. And her scream."

Molly squeezed his hand. "E.J…"

He shook his head.

"It wasn't her. It was Johnny. A police officer responding to the call shot him. He was still alive when they cuffed him, but he bled out on the way to the hospital."

His voice faded.

"And Jane… she changed that day. Something left her. She was never the same."

The lake lapped quietly beneath them.

"I thought I could protect her," E.J. whispered. "I thought I could protect everyone."

Molly leaned against his shoulder.

"I'm so sorry," she said. "For all of it."

E.J. didn't answer right away. He just looked out at the darkening water.

"That's what you saw in my eyes that day," he finally said. "That wreckage. That shadow."

"I saw someone who still cares," Molly said. "Who's trying to find light again."

He turned to her, grateful.

"I didn't want to keep it from you. I just… didn't know how to say it."

"I get it," she said.

They stayed like that as the last of the sunlight bled into the lake. And for the first time in a long time, the weight on E.J.'s chest began to ease.

CHAPTER TWENTY-SEVEN — *Healing*

Tyler didn't want to be here, it was too early. He wanted to be asleep—curled beneath a blanket, far from the world and its noise. But instead, he sat in a gray folding chair in the Castleton Community Center, beneath fluorescent lights that buzzed like they were tired, too. The room was circular, the kind that made it hard to disappear.

Court-ordered counseling. Anger management. Violence prevention.

He scanned the circle—six or so faces, none of them familiar. Some were hollow-eyed. Some just tired. No one looked ready to speak.

The facilitator sat forward slightly, his voice calm but not soft.

"Who here can tell me what accountability means to them?" he asked. "Not the dictionary definition. Yours. What does it feel like? What does it look like?"

Silence.

A beat passed. Then another.

Tyler looked around again. Still nothing.

So he spoke.

Not because he had to. But because… maybe he needed to.

"It feels like standing still," he said, voice low but audible. "Like facing yourself in the mirror after everyone's walked away."

A few heads turned his direction.

Tyler swallowed and continued.

"I used to think I was born angry. Like it was stitched into me. Like it didn't matter what I did, it would always come back out somehow." He paused, breath catching slightly. "But that's a lie I told myself to avoid doing the work."

The room stayed quiet.

"I hurt someone I care about," he said. "And it could've been worse. That's the part that keeps me up some nights. I scared people. I scared myself."

He exhaled.

"But I don't want to be that person again."

The facilitator nodded slowly.

"What person do you want to be?" he asked.

Tyler didn't hesitate.

"Someone they feel safe around. Someone who doesn't spiral. Someone who knows who he is… and still chooses not to hurt people."

A silence followed—thick, but not cold.

It wasn't applause. It wasn't forgiveness.

But maybe it was the beginning.

He stared down at the floor from his seat.

Dillon stared up at the ceiling. His mind wouldn't stop racing from his bed.

A slow blink.

And then—

FLASH

That night by the lake. Paige's lips, warm from firelight, pressed gently against his. Her fingers tangled with his under the stars.

FLASH

The back porch.

"Surprise!"

Everyone cheering. Paige turning, stunned, then spotting him above her on the back porch. That look—wide-eyed, full of light. He ran down the steps, kissed her like he meant it. Because he did.

FLASH

Brady's Ice Cream. The sun in her eyes, her laugh tangled in a bite of butter pecan. Her hand looped into his. "Take the picture," she said. And he did, camera flashing…

Back in his room.

Dillon blinked again. Reality felt dimmer.

He pulled his phone from under the blanket. Opened Photos.

There they were. That same picture—Paige squinting at the sun, smiling like the world couldn't touch her.

He whispered to the room, "How did everything go so wrong?"

A buzz vibrated in his hand.

KEEGAN: *Come hop in the pool. Last warm days left.*

Dillon let out a breath of a laugh. He typed back:

DILLON: *Be there later.*

When the message sent, the picture returned, Paige's smile and he was the lucky guy to be beside her.

He stood. The phone stayed on the bed.

The light through the window shifted across the room as he walked toward the bathroom—each step feeling like maybe, just maybe, something was shifting with him.

The late morning sun brushed against the edges of the Winthrop backyard.

E.J. and Molly lay together in the hammock, slow-swaying under the weight of the day and all that had come before it. Somewhere, a neighbor's wind chime clinked lazily in the breeze.

Molly shifted slightly, her head nestled just below his collarbone.

"Thank you," she said softly. "For trusting me with everything."

E.J.'s arm tightened around her. His chest rose and fell in a measured breath.

"It's weird," he said, eyes fixed on the leaves overhead. "After all this time… it actually feels lighter. Like carrying that story around made everything feel heavier. And now—" he paused "—I don't know. I finally feel like I'm breathing again."

Molly looked up at him. "That's what happens when you let someone in."

He nodded faintly. But then his jaw set—not in anger, but in worry.

"There's something off about Jane," he said. "At first, she grieved quietly. Wouldn't talk much. But now… it's like something cracked. Like she's trying to become someone else just to avoid feeling anything at all."

"She doesn't seem like herself," Molly admitted.

"She's not," E.J. replied. "And maybe she hasn't been for a while."

They lay there in silence, the world exhaling around them.

"I'm going on the camping trip," E.J. added. "I need to keep an eye on her."

Molly tilted her chin up again.

"You sure you're ready for that? After everything?"

"I wasn't there for her when it mattered most," he said. "I can't change that. But I can be there now."

Before Molly could answer, Mrs. Winthrop's voice carried out from the back door.

"Time to start loading the car!"

Molly smiled softly. "That's our cue."

E.J. lingered a moment longer, his fingers brushing hers.

This time, when the hammock rocked—it felt less like drifting, and more like forward motion.

CHAPTER TWENTY-EIGHT — *Something Broke*

The late afternoon sun filtered through the trees in fractured beams, streaking the campsite in dusty gold. A portable speaker buzzed low with music as zippers zipped and tent poles clattered into place.

"I'm just saying," Maria said, struggling with a corner stake, "this is exactly how every horror movie starts."

"Right?" Sam grinned. "Legend says some woman and her daughter were out here years ago—and only one of them made it back."

"Supposedly," Maria added, drawing it out. "Evil spirits in the woods."

Molly gave a mock shiver, as Sam sarcastically responded. "Love that for us."

Jane rolled her eyes from behind her half-assembled tent. "You people are so dramatic."

Next to Jane, E.J., crouched beside his and Molly's nearly finished tent, smirking. "Says the girl who brought contour to a campsite."

Jane flipped her curls. "It's called being camera-ready."

Her lashes were full, her lip gloss perfect, her expression anything but amused. Combat boots. Cropped hoodie. Black leggings.

E.J. eyed her, before putting the final stake his and Molly's tent.

"Done," he said.

E.J. walked over to Jane's tent, much further behind in assembly, crouching to secure a loose panel. "Need help?"

Jane sighed like it physically hurt her to accept it. "Why do people willingly do this?"

"Camping?" E.J. asked. "Pretty sure this was your idea."

Jane flipped her hair over her shoulder, irritation flashing behind her eyes. As Molly joined them, Jane's gaze landed on her. Then on E.J. again. Something unreadable lingered there—cool, distant.

"Well," Jane muttered, slipping out her phone and turning her back, "looks like guys got it from here."

Across the clearing, Sam and Maria leaned against their own tent, watching.

"There's something off with her," Maria said under her breath.

Sam nodded. "Ever since that night she danced out my sunroof."

"No," Maria replied, eyes narrowed. "Even before. Remember the pool? That outburst about Heather? That wasn't Jane."

A gust of wind lifted leaves off the forest floor. Jane began walking from the tents straight towards the heavily forested trees.

"Where are you going?" E.J. called.

Jane didn't look back. "I need to be alone."

Molly stepped forward to E.J. "That's not a good idea. She doesn't even know the woods—she could get lost."

E.J.'s shoulders tensed. "Something's not right."

Molly studied him. "You're always looking out for her."

"I wasn't there before," E.J. said, already stepping forward, "but I'll be there now."

He jogged after Jane, weaving into the trees.

Sam and Maria hurried over. "What happened?" Maria asked.

"She took off," Molly said, scanning the treeline. "E.J.'s going after her. Something's definitely wrong."

In the woods, the world grew quieter. Shadows thickened between the trunks. The air cooled. Jane walked like the forest had opened for her and she didn't need permission. Leaves crackled beneath her boots. The scent of pine and old smoke lingered.

Then—through the trees—she saw it.

A structure, or what was left of one. Charred beams. A collapsed interior. A skeleton of a house blackened by fire and time. Ash coated the ground like gray snow.

A rusted mailbox leaned at the edge of the path.

The name was barely legible beneath the rust, but still there:
STANDISH

Jane blinked hard.

Then a voice.

Her voice. But wrong.

"You can't keep me hiding in here forever."

Jane turned sharply. No one was there. Just trees. The wind.

"I'm stronger now," the voice whispered, curling inside her like smoke. "And I want out."

"No," Jane hissed.

"You've pushed me down long enough."

"Shut up," she said louder, her pulse hammering. "I'm in control now, you had your chance."

"Are you?"

Jane clutched her head. "STOP IT!" she screamed. "Get out of my head!"

Her voice cracked through the trees, high and fractured.

E.J. paused.

He heard it—her scream, sharp and raw. Panic gripped him. He bolted forward, brushing past branches and hopping fallen limbs.

"Jane?" he shouted.

No answer.

Just the wind and the forest breathing, the sky darkening.

He ran harder until the trees opened. The burned house loomed before him—an open wound in the woods.

He slowed. His chest rose and fell. He scanned the clearing.

No sign of her.

"Jane," he called again, lower this time. Urgent. "It's me."

But the forest only echoed his voice back in fragments.

She was already farther ahead.

And he had no idea what she was walking into.

Back at the campsite, the sky had turned from amber to gray, the temperature cooling.

Maria looked up from her seat on a log. "Do you think they're alright out there?"

Molly stood near the tents, arms crossed tightly. She glanced at the horizon, where daylight was quickly draining away.

"I don't know," she said. "But I'm worried."

She grabbed a flashlight from the supply bin and flicked it on. A pale beam of light cut through the dim.

"We need to get them back. Now."

Without hesitation, Maria and Sam each grabbed one too. No words, just shared urgency.

They moved fast, weaving into the trees, flashlights bouncing with every step. The air grew cooler, the sound of crickets beginning to rise around them.

Deeper in the forest, Jane moved like a ghost—barely tethered to the ground. Her boots struck wet leaves and twigs, but her mind was somewhere else entirely.

The voice was louder now. Fierce.

"I'm stronger now."

"You're not real!" Jane shouted into the dark.

Thunder cracked above the trees.

She stopped, her body stiff. The world felt like it was closing in, like something inside her was clawing to get out. Her breath came in short bursts, her vision splintered.

"NO!" she screamed.

Somewhere behind, E.J. heard it.

He broke into a run.

Branches whipped against his arms, his legs burning as he pushed forward, faster, faster—

"Jane!"

He spotted her—just ahead, on unstable ground.

"Jane—wait!"

But she turned too sharply. One wrong step—

CRACK.

The forest floor gave way beneath her.

With a sharp scream, she fell—vanishing into the dark below.

"JANE!"

E.J. dove forward, barely catching the edge. Dirt crumbled beneath his fingers as he stared into the jagged, black hole in the earth. A collapsed mine shaft, its opening barely visible until it was too late.

"JANE!" he screamed again, panic lacing his voice.

In the distance, Molly skidded to a halt as she heard him.

"Did you hear that?" she gasped.

Sam and Maria nodded in sync.

Then they ran.

Toward the voice.

Toward the scream.

Toward whatever came next.

CHAPTER TWENTY-NINE — *Dark Divide*

Thunder cracked above the trees like the sky was splitting open. Light rain began to fall in thin sheets, slicing through the branches overhead.

E.J. knelt at the mouth of the shaft, shouting her name over and over. "Jane! JANE!" But there was no answer—only the wind howling through the forest.

Molly skidded to a stop behind him. "What happened?"

"She fell," he choked out, eyes wild. "The ground just... gave way. It's a shaft—an old mine, I think."

Maria and Sam arrived next, breathless, faces blanching as they saw the jagged pit. Sam pulled out his phone in the rain. "No signal," he muttered.

"Then we're on our own," E.J. said, wiping water from his face.

Sam's mind raced. "My mom packed rope. She bought gear— literally everything, there's got to be something back at the camp we can use."

"We have to go back!" E.J. snapped.

He and Sam bolted through the rain, breathless.

Maria dropped to her knees at the edge, flashlight beam trembling in her hand. "Jane! Can you hear me?"

Below, she saw her—laying still, unmoving.

Molly knelt beside her, hands folded, whispering a prayer. "Please be okay. Please."

Beneath the Earth

In the silence of the shaft, Jane lay unmoving.

But in her mind—it was loud.

A black void stretched endlessly around her. She stood in the darkness, the emptiness—wild curls, smeared eyeliner, a twisted grin —arms crossed.

"Thought you were getting out?" she cackled. "Not so fast, original recipe."

Then—a tap on her shoulder.

She turned, startled. And there she was—again. Her real self. This version composed, hair tied back in a sleek ponytail, cardigan pristine, eyes fierce.

"I told you I was stronger," the proper Jane said coldly. "You locked me up… but I got out."

"You can't. I locked you in myself."

"I'm Jane, you're not."

For the first time, the curly-haired version seemed frightened— shocked that her alter was strong enough to get from behind bars.

Then—

The proper Jane shoved her backward—forceful, unrelenting— like the devil herself was falling into the abyss, crashing backward into a black sea with a deafening SPLASH that swallowed her whole. Screaming. Thrashing. Then sinking, soundlessly.

The void flickered.

Above, voices echoed through the dark.

"Jane!"

"JANE!"

"Come on, Jane—wake up!"

E.J. … Molly … Sam … Maria.

Her people.

Her eyes fluttered open. Dirt. Cold. Rain streaming. Lashes heavy. Shapes above her—blurred by water and panic.

"Jane!" E.J.'s voice cracked.

He was descending, rain harder, soaked to the bone, the rope cutting into his waist. The storm swirled around them, the line trembling under tension.

He reached her, dropping to his knees. Her body lay twisted, dazed, her hand barely twitching.

"Hey, hey—look at me," E.J. whispered, pulling her into his arms. "I've got you."

She blinked, dazed, eyes locking with his for a heartbeat. Her brother… her savior.

She whispered, "E.J…."

He held her—tight. It felt like the first time he'd truly held his sister in months. Like she wasn't made of glass anymore. Like she was real.

"I'm here," he breathed. "I'm not letting go."

Above, Sam, Maria and Molly braced the rope as it creaked—strained. One more pull and—

SNAP.

"Jesus, no!" Molly screamed, her knuckles white around the grip.

E.J. felt it give. He looked up, fear surging.

"Pull slower!" Maria shouted. "Steady!"

The rope fraying by its fibers, separating.

The teens pulled—inch by inch. E.J. wrapped his body around Jane's, shielding her, whispering through the rain.

"You're okay. We're almost there. Just a little more."

Finally—hands reached down. Molly and Maria. E.J. pushed upward and Jane was lifted free, muddy and slick, onto the forest floor as Sam continued to harness up E.J.

Jane lay on the ground… still.

Molly dropped to her knees beside her. "Jane? Jane?"

"C'mon, Jane." Sam's voice cracked. "Stay with us."

But she didn't respond.

The storm swallowed them all, lightning splitting the sky as they hovered around her, soaked, trembling. E.J. ran next to his sister.

And still—Jane didn't move.

She was out cold.

CHAPTER THIRTY — *Eye of the Storm*

The hospital room was dim, lit only by the rhythmic glow of the heart monitor and the gray light of the storm beyond the window. E.J. sat in the chair beside Jane's bed, unmoving. His hand rested near hers, not quite touching—afraid to disturb the stillness.

She still hadn't woken.

Her face was pale against the white pillow, hair damp around her temples, a faint bruise blooming just beneath her cheekbone. He leaned forward, elbows on knees, voice low.

"Hang in there, okay? I'm not going anywhere," he said.

Behind him, Sam and Maria stood quietly near the door, watching. The beeping monitor filled the room like breath. Then—Sam's phone buzzed. He glanced down.

TYLER: How's the camping trip?

He stared at the message, thumb hovering, unsure how to respond.

Inside Prescott Estate, Tyler looked down at his phone—the message finally showed sent, a delay due to the storm. Then he set it aside.

He sat inside the living room, the rain cascading down the wide glass doors that framed the backyard pool. The storm had rolled in fast, swallowing what was supposed to be the last golden afternoon of summer.

Tyler sat on one end of the L-shaped sectional, swim trunks still damp. Dillon, Paige, Keegan, and Heather were sprawled nearby, all soaked and drying off with towels. The scent of chlorine clung faintly to the air.

Dillon spoke first. "Well. At least we got a swim in before the sky lost its mind."

"Seriously," Paige said, tucking wet curls behind her ear.

Keegan groaned, glancing toward the downpour. "It didn't say rain when I checked this morning. This freak storm came out of the blue."

Dillon glanced at Paige. She looked back. Brief. Barely a second. But something passed between them—soft, unsure, almost… hopeful.

Keegan caught it.

"I'm gonna go grab drinks," he said, pushing up from the couch with a casual smirk.

Dillon followed. "I'll help."

They disappeared into the kitchen, their voices fading with distance.

In the kitchen—

"Why didn't you tell me Paige would be here?" Dillon said as he leaned against the counter.

Keegan opened the fridge. "Oh, come on. Don't act like you're not happy to see her."

Dillon cracked the smallest smile. "I mean, I am. I just… wasn't ready."

"Sure you were," Keegan said, handing him a couple of cans. "You've been ready. Just scared."

Dillon grabbed the drinks, but his eyes stayed on Keegan. "And what about you and Heather?"

A beat.

"I'm right here," Heather said from the kitchen doorway, leaning against the frame, towel wrapped around her shoulders, her voice dry.

Dillon blinked. "Well… I'll just take these and disappear." He lifted the drinks and made a graceful exit.

Now alone, Keegan looked at Heather. She didn't move.

"I'm glad you came," he said, sincerely.

"Couldn't say no to sun and fun," she replied, then looked at the storm through the window. "Even if it only lasted a second."

They both laughed—lightly, genuinely.

She turned to him. "So. What've you learned since we split?"

Keegan sobered, leaning back against the counter. "Not to be a dick. And not to take for granted what's right in front of me."

Heather raised an eyebrow.

"I mean it," he said. "None of the other stuff meant anything. You and me—we were something. And I was stupid enough to forget that."

Heather crossed her arms, not yet yielding. "Words are easy, Keegan. You've always been good with those."

"Then let me show you. With actions," he said. "Does that mean I get a second chance?"

She studied him, long enough that the silence almost felt dangerous. Then—she smirked.

"Maybe."

Behind them, the rain poured harder—steady, relentless, alive with tension.

CHAPTER THIRTY-ONE — *Drip*

The rain had stopped.

From the balcony off Keegan's bedroom, Paige and Heather sat cross-legged on the damp tile, backs against the wall. A soft drip echoed above them, steady water sliding off the edge of the roof. Below, the town of Castleton twinkled—golden porch lights and streetlamps stretching like scattered stars across the hills.

The night was calm. Quiet. A brief breath after everything.

"I can't believe we're about to be seniors," Paige said, her voice low. "Like, next week we'll be walking those halls again. One last time."

Heather rested her chin on her knees, eyes fixed on the view. "You going to senior sunrise?"

Paige nodded slowly. "I wouldn't miss it, its tradition. Even after the craziest summer of our lives."

She leaned her head onto Heather's shoulder, letting her words hang in the cooling air.

"I love you, Heather Briarwood," she whispered. "You've been a constant since I moved here. And I want you to remember that you're irreplaceable."

Heather didn't look at her. Just kept staring out over the town as a tear slipped down one cheek.

"I'll remember that," she said.

The glass door behind them slid open.

"Ladies," Keegan said, stepping out with a soft grin. "Hope I'm not interrupting."

Heather turned, wiped her cheek quickly, and smiled. "Just girl chat," she said with a laugh.

Paige stood, brushing off her shorts. "I'll leave you two at it."

Downstairs, Dillon sat on the couch, thumbs idly scrolling on his phone, still half-damp from the storm. When he looked up, Paige had come down the stairs, walking into the living room—hair a little frizzy.

"What're you doing?" she asked.

Dillon's eyes lit up just a little. "Thought you left."

"Still here," she said, stepping closer.

He set his phone aside. "Tyler already took off."

"Then I guess we're the only ones down here."

She climbed onto his lap, straddling him.

"I know we went wrong somewhere," Paige said. "But I don't want that to be our story. Not going into senior year."

Dillon steadied her waist, their faces inches apart.

"So what does that mean for us?"

She tilted her head. "What do you want it to mean?"

He didn't hesitate. "That we see each other again. Really see each other. And that you see yourself, too."

Paige's eyes searched his.

"You're gorgeous, Paige," Dillon said. "And people will talk, people will judge, likely because they're jealous. But don't let them decide your worth. You're perfect the way you are. And I want to be with you for a reason."

Her lip trembled. "Do you mean that?"

"I do. And I need you to remember it. Through everything. I never stopped caring about you."

Then he kissed her. She kissed him back. And for a moment, they weren't just two teens caught in the drama of a chaotic summer—they were just them. Real. Reconnected. Whole.

Drip.

The IV in Jane's hospital room let out a soft click every few seconds. Steady. Reassuring.

E.J. sat beside her, his hand wrapped loosely around hers. Machines beeped softly. The fluorescent lights above were dimmed, casting the room in a soft glow.

"Mom and Dad are on their way," he whispered.

He leaned forward, forehead nearly touching her knuckles.

"I'm not going anywhere."

Outside the room, through the hallway window, Sam and Maria stood watching. Still damp from the rain, their clothes clinging lightly to their skin.

"We've had a crazy-ass summer," Maria said softly.

Sam exhaled. "I'm actually looking forward to school starting. Something about going back to normalcy... sounds kind of nice."

Maria didn't answer right away.

Then—

"Sam, look!"

They both froze.

Inside, Jane stirred. A twitch in her fingers. Her eyes blinked once… twice…

They rushed in.

E.J. was already leaning over her, the relief on his face like sunrise after a long night.

Jane turned to him, weak but aware.

"Thank you," she whispered. "For saving me."

He smiled, tears slipping down without shame.

"I love you," she said.

"I love you too," he whispered, "so much."

Outside, the rain had stopped. But inside, healing had finally begun.

CHAPTER THIRTY-TWO — *The Letter*

A few days later, the morning light spilled in through the narrow windows of the Castleton Community Center, softer than usual. Tyler sat quietly in his folding chair—same circle, same scuffed linoleum floors, same buzzing ceiling light. But something felt different.

He'd been here before. Too many times. The chairs were always too hard, the coffee always burned, the stories shared never easy. But slowly, this room had taught him things.

Today, the counselor passed around a sheet of paper and spoke simply.

"Write a letter," he said. "To the person you hurt. Be honest. Be human. Don't worry about forgiveness. Just be true."

Tyler stared at the page for a long time.

Then he picked up his pen and wrote:

I was angry at myself. At the world for not making sense. I didn't know where to put it, so I handed it to you—and that wasn't fair. I'm sorry I scared you. I'm sorry I gave you reasons not to trust me. You didn't deserve that.

He sat back, exhaling, the weight of his own words he'd started to write sat heavy—but clean.

A few blocks away, Molly sat cross-legged on her bed, still in a tank top and cotton shorts, eyes scanning the backyard through her window.

Down below, next-door at the Winthrop's, E.J. and Jane lay in the hammock, swaying slightly in the breeze. Their legs tangled, the canvas swinging gently like breath.

Jane looked smaller than usual in E.J.'s hoodie, her hair half-dried from a recent shower. She stared out at the garden, quiet.

E.J. nudged her. "They found pills in your system."

Jane didn't flinch. "They helped," she murmured. "Until they didn't."

He looked at her. "Where'd they come from?"

She hesitated. "Johnny. Just something to take the edge off, he said. Back when things were first getting bad."

E.J. stilled. She continued.

"I thought if I couldn't feel anything, I couldn't fall apart again."

She pulled the sleeves over her hands, voice barely above a whisper. "And then… the text."

"What text?"

Her jaw tensed. "*I know your secret.* I sent it. To myself."

E.J.'s eyes widened.

"I didn't realize it at first," she said. "I was dissociating—just gone. And when I saw it later, I thought someone else had sent it. I freaked. It didn't cause the spiral… but it definitely sent it into overdrive."

E.J. turned to face her fully, eyes soft with heartbreak.

"You don't have to be okay all the time," he said gently. "But you don't have to carry it alone either."

A long beat. Then—

"I love you," Jane whispered, chin trembling.

E.J. wrapped her in his arms, kissing the top of her head.

"I love you more. Always."

Upstairs, Molly turned from the window and pulled her diary from the nightstand. She opened to a fresh page and began to write:

Things in Castleton are starting to look up.

What started as a crazy summer now has me hopeful for senior year. I've made new friends. Had new experiences. I don't know what's coming—but I want it all. Homecoming. Prom. Graduation. Memories that actually mean something.

And maybe… drama-free this time.

She closed the book and pulled off her locket. The clasp clicked gently. Inside was a picture—her and her mom, forehead to forehead, smiling.

She ran a thumb across the glass.

"I love you," she whispered.

Somewhere across town, a folded letter sat in a counselor's outbox, waiting to be sent.

CHAPTER THIRTY-THREE — *Anticipation*

For the first time in what felt like forever, Castleton's postcard beauty seemed to shine brighter. Sunlight spilled down sleepy streets. Even ordinary life began to feel possible again.

At Sam's house, he and Maria stepped out the kitchen door into the driveway, both dressed in matching athleisure—like a campaign ad for "new year, new us."

"We should've started this weeks ago," Maria said, tightening her ponytail.

Sam snorted. "We were kind of busy with, you know… trauma."

They laughed.

Just then, a man walked up the driveway toward them as they climbed into the red Honda Civic. Trim beard, calm eyes, a Castleton Community Center lanyard around his neck.

"Marcus," he said, flashing a kind smile. "I facilitate the violence prevention sessions. Someone asked me to give you this."

He handed Sam a sealed envelope.

"Take care of yourself," Marcus added, and walked off.

Sam just sat there, staring at the letter. Like it might burn through his fingers.

A few blocks away, Molly shut her mailbox at the curb just as a pair of hands slipped a Castleton High School letterman jacket over her shoulders from behind. The Hellcat stitched on the back looked ready to pounce.

She turned, smiling already.

"You can't be the only girl at senior sunrise without school spirit," E.J. said.

"I love it," she whispered, grabbing his collar and pulling him into a kiss right there on the lawn.

Next door, Jane stood at the Winthrop mailbox collecting her own mail.

"Hey," Molly called. "How are you doing?"

Jane shrugged, but there was more light behind her eyes than there'd been in weeks. "Signed up for varsity cheer. Hoping I make the cut."

"That's so cool," Molly said, grinning. E.J. gave a subtle, proud nod from behind her.

Jane smirked. "Guess we're all finding our way back. By the way, Molly—we still need to do that girls' day, just the two of us."

Molly smiled.

Downtown, Paige and Heather moved through the racks of a boutique, flipping through hangers with dangerous precision.

Paige held up a white eyelet dress. "Too soft?"

Heather held up a slinky black mini. "Too soft for who?"

Paige blinked. "That's for senior sunrise?"

Heather laughed. "No, silly. Keegan planned a whole thing for tonight—dinner at the Lobster Shack. Candlelight, reservations, the whole thing."

Paige smirked. "Bougie. You better get the bread. It's the best part."

Outside, a blur sped past the shop window.

Molly clung to E.J.'s back as he rode them through Castleton on his bike. She laughed into the breeze, hair whipping behind her as they passed the Castleton Community Center, then the Burger Hut, Brady's Ice Cream, Jerry's Fitness Club, and finally, the open sweep of Raven Lake, sparkling under the sun.

"This finally feels like home," she whispered in his ear.

E.J. smiled without turning around. "That's because it is."

Later that day, evening folded in slow, warm.

Inside the Powell house, Tyler stood in front of a mirror in the bedroom, pulling at the collar of a clean shirt.

"I can't believe this fits," he said, half to himself.

Dillon let out a soft laugh from where he sat on the edge of his bed, a pile of clothes beside him. "I don't wear half this stuff anymore —my arms can't fit. These were before my gains."

Tyler laughed, grateful.

"Besides, Tyler—you start at the Burger Hut next week. You'll have your own drip soon."

Tyler nodded, but a sense of sadness crossed his face for a split second. Dillon caught it.

"What's wrong?" Dillon asked.

A pause.

"Still no word from my folks, even after all this time."

Mr. Powell appeared at the bedroom door, voice calm and rooted. "You've got us. We're your family now."

Tyler nodded slowly, a smile tugging at his lips.

Then—a knock at the front door.

Dillon disappeared to answer it.

Tyler continued staring in the mirror.

Then—

"Tyler," Dillon called from the front of the house. "It's for you."

Tyler rounded the corner—and froze.

Sam stood in the doorway. He held the now-open letter in one hand.

Tyler's breath hitched. "I thought… the court order—"

Sam cut in. "I signed a waiver. The no-contact order isn't a thing anymore."

Tyler glanced at his letter in Sam's hand.

"Even before the letter," Sam said, eyes tearing. "I knew I couldn't go another second without seeing you."

And then he stepped forward, closer to Tyler.

They kissed. Not careful. Not rehearsed. Just real.

The living room dimmed around them as the night settled in.

Tomorrow was senior sunrise.

But tonight?

Tonight felt like magic.

EPILOGUE — *Senior Sunrise*

The sun hadn't quite risen yet, but it was the first day of school. At Castleton High, a new class of seniors gathered on the football field, as tradition called for—early, bleary-eyed, and full of quiet anticipation. Folding tables lined the track, offering muffins, orange juice, granola bars, and other sleepy fare. The smell of cinnamon and citrus drifted through the morning air, carried inland on a breeze from Raven Lake.

Keegan had brought his own speakers from home, that thumped with the pulse of Bryce Vine's "The Kids Aren't Alright," offering the crowd something upbeat to wake to. More seniors arrived by the minute, hugging hello, tucking into breakfast with laughter that felt like promise.

From the sideline, next to his speaker, Keegan caught Heather's eye on the bleachers and smiled. Her hair blew lightly in the wind.

Next to her sat Paige, serene in a sleeveless white dress. Dillon approached and, without a word, draped his jacket over her shoulders. She leaned into him, her hand curling into his.

Above them, E.J. sat beside Molly, her hoodie zipped to her chin. She unlocked her phone and lifted it just as the sun began to break the horizon, spilling gold across the field and bringing the Hellcat mascot at midfield to life.

Maria smiled at Sam beside her, and he smiled back.

Then—movement beneath the bleachers caught Sam's eye.

Tyler had arrived, uncertain, hands in the sleeves of a borrowed hoodie. Sam stood. He called to him—quiet, sure—and extended a hand. Tyler climbed up. Sat beside him. Sam's arm wrapped around him as naturally as breath.

Together, they watched the sun rise.

Across town, on the roof outside her window— Jane, sat wrapped in a blanket, knees hugged to her chest. She watched the golden light spill across rooftops and treetops, stretching toward the horizon like something sacred.

She exhaled—long and slow.

For the first time in a long time, she believed it.

Everything was going to be okay.

FADE TO LIGHT